Chandi and the Pearl of Making

A Shattered Moon Novel

Suzi Yee

Text Copyright © 2019 by Suzi Yee

Published by Expeditious Retreat Press
Cover by Vivid Covers
Edited by Elizabeth VanZwolle

For information regarding Suzi Yee's novels and to subscribe to her mailing list, see her website at https://www.joseph-browning.com

To follow Suzi on Twitter: https://twitter.com/Joseph_Browning

To follow Suzi on Facebook: https://www.facebook.com/SuziYeeAuthor

To follow Suzi on MeWee: https://mewe.com/i/josephbrowning

By Suzi Yee

SHATTERED MOON NOVELS: CHANDI SERIES
Chandi and the Moonstone
Chandi and the Pearl of Making
Chandi and the Black Diamond

Chapter One

Chandi burrowed deeper under her bedclothes, staving off the bitter chill of early morning. When the trapped warmth of her body was almost too much to bear, she would pop her head out for ventilation. The rush of cold air was both a relief and an excuse to stay in bed a little longer. As the days shortened and the temperatures dropped, Chandi had more and more mornings like this. The rooster's crow came later and later, and once harvest was complete, the pace of life would slow at the Monastery of Unseen Waters. Unfortunately, Chandi had to cut this morning short. She had a promise to keep.

"It's your turn today," Lucy called from the top bunk, her words slightly slurred from sleep. "You can bed-pig tomorrow."

Chandi let out a groan as she pulled on her clothes under the covers; getting dressed in the warmth made it slightly less an affront. She reluctantly relinquished the weighty coziness of her blankets as she left her bed and quickly splashed clean water from the basin onto her face, shocking the last of slumber's haze out of her almond-shaped green eyes. She brushed the tangles that somehow formed in the night out of her hair before braiding and fastening her black locks into place. Adding a few more layers before venturing out, Chandi left her roommate—snug in the relative heat of their room—and headed out to the courtyard.

To Sura's credit, she was there, ready and waiting as Chandi braced herself against the brisk breeze. The petite blonde was bundled up and rubbing her mitten-covered hands together. "Remind me why we have to do this first thing in the morning?" she greeted Chandi.

"Because if we waited until after dinner, you'd never do it. It gives you too much time to find a reason not to," the pathfinder answered as she stretched her body and got her blood moving. "Plus, your muscles don't get as tired when it's cold outside. But that doesn't mean you can skip warming up…" Chandi nudged the tenderfoot to follow her lead.

The Church of Parkour selected young sentients with exceptional special abilities to train as runners at the Monastery of Unseen Waters, so it was ironic that Sura detested running as a general rule. Still, if she ever wanted to leave the ranks of tenderfoots and join her friends in novice training, she had to get tough. It didn't matter how good she became at the other maneuvers, if she didn't have the stamina to run.

Which is where her friends came in. Sura didn't have the endurance to run very long during afternoon training, so Chandi, Lucy, Hanu, and Willem—after a little prodding from Lucy—took turns running with her in the morning. The theory seemed sound: if she couldn't run a long distance at once, run shorter courses multiple times a day until she could eventually manage a longer course.

Sura quickly learned how to improve her form, run more efficiently, and pace herself. She also picked up snippets about her newly found friends. Willem liked to play instructor, pointing out every little thing he was and wasn't doing. Lucy sensed when Sura was getting tired or disheartened and offered encouragement when the tenderfoot hit her nadir. Hanu was playful, turning morning runs into a prolonged game of chase or tag. Chandi taught her it was possible for one to find serenity in running, even if Sura couldn't muster such inner stillness between her aching legs and burning lungs.

Chandi was dead silent when she ran—not just the lack of conversation, but also in her motion. Sometimes Sura had to look sideways to make sure her companion was still nearby. Every once in a while, Chandi would offer a correction, but otherwise she let Sura find her path. *Every runner must run at their own pace; as is it written, so it is run.*

As their breath and bodies thawed, the runners shed layers and found their stride. As they rounded one corner of the inner perimeter, an Order of the Guard sentry waved at their passing, as much to let them know they were seen as out of courtesy. Their patrols had been more diligent after the events of the summer and the looming wars of Dexter Albert Winchester VI, ruler of the Kingdom of a Thousand Islands and beneficent charterer of the Watertown ruins to the Church of Parkour. While most of the fighting was happening on the kingdom's eastern and southern borders, Dexter was still technically at war with the Lordship of Fingers to the west, and hostilities had a way of spilling over the land as all available food and resources were funneled into the machinery of war.

As they completed one lap, Chandi looked over to Sura. Her cheeks were flush, but her breathing held steady and she was holding her form. Chandi smiled. Only a few months before, this had been Sura's absolute limit. *We'll make a runner out of you yet*, she thought to herself as she picked up the pace.

As much as Chandi grumbled getting out of bed, running in the morning wasn't all that bad—she found it easier to still her mind during morning devotion afterward, and the hot bowl of porridge at breakfast was tastier than normal. Now past the jarring events of summer, the entire monastery was blissfully bustling like normal through autumn's harvest and food preservation, with a notable absence of spirits-made-flesh and mutated ruin horrors.

Everyone had their own theories about the return to relative normalcy. The fatalistic chalked it up as part of the natural ebb and flow of chaos under the shattered moon, often without rhyme or reason but with serious consequences nonetheless. The religious felt it was a test—could we run fast enough to escape *this* time? Others placed their faith in Jackson, Unseen Water's resident sorcerer, and his diligent work repairing and improving the monastery's dusty wards. The thinkers were unwilling to weigh in on the matter, citing insufficient data to support any one theory over another. Khiri, the tigrine abbess, was certain that getting Moonstone out of the monastery played no small part.

Chandi was of two minds about the entire affair. She couldn't dispute Moonstone's causality, but that didn't mean she was entirely convinced the acts were purposefully malevolent. The practical part of her acknowledged that when it came to cause and disastrous effect, intention did little to mitigate the damage, but her strong streak of fairness couldn't relinquish the notion that motivation counted for something.

And so the day unfolded. All hands were involved in drying, canning, salting, and curing the fruits of all their labors up to now. Students of all levels meditated through movement, and evening came ever sooner as the days grew shorter. Dinner was a hearty stew fortified with bone broth, along with heavy loaves of bread. Conversation around the communal tables centered on matters mundane: the harvest, the weather, accounts of the trials and tribulations encountered during meditations, and gossip about the current scholars and tracers visiting the Monastery of Unseen Waters.

After a long day and with her early start, Chandi was satisfied, listening to the chatter of her companions. Willem was humble-bragging about his latest find in the ruins; he really did have a knack for spotting small shiny things of value.

Hanu was contemplating how one would liberate a few jars of jam for later personal use; this year's yield was so good, surely they wouldn't miss one or two? Sura was actually excited about running, namely because her instructors had finally cleared her to advance to novice training. Lucy was consumed with planning for the Longest Night—well over a month away—but as far as Lucy was concerned, it was never too early to start plotting.

Many of the holidays of the ancients were observed under the shattered moon, but the Church of Parkour was sparing in its holy days. One notable exception was the celebration of winter solstice, referred to as the Longest Night by those of the faith. Officially, it marked the beginning of winter, a period of reflection before a new cycle of renewal began in spring. In practice, it was an evening when the systematic formality of the church was relaxed, and celebrated with a bonfire, mulled cider, and small gifts.

The entire main hall would be lit as a beacon against the darkness as the abbess led the monastery in the traditional rite of observance, performed to ensure that spring would come again. Chandi secretly found it ironic that an institution focused on escaping the cycle of reincarnation under the shattered moon was so invested in the cycle of the seasons continuing without fail, but she had learned over time that such thoughts were best kept to oneself.

"Earth to Chandi?" Lucy snapped her fingers in front of

the blank stare on her roommate's face.

"What?" Chandi broke out of her reverie.

"I asked if you were going to see Brother Bartholomew tonight."

"I was planning to. Why?"

"He told me he found something to make this year's Longest Night decorations really sparkle, and I was wondering if you wouldn't mind me coming with you."

Chandi shrugged her slim shoulders before smearing the last of her bread with fruit compote. "Sure, why not?"

In retrospect, Chandi should have realized something was up—the speed with which Hanu, Willem, and Sura simultaneously cleared the dinner table, Lucy's insistence that they needed to go back to their room before heading to Brother Bartholomew's, and the inordinate amount of time she spent brushing her hair before they left. Something finally pinged on Chandi's radar as they were approaching the scholar's door and Lucy's voice grew progressively louder.

Chandi's eyes narrowed suspiciously. "What's going on, Lucy?"

"I don't know what you are talking about," Lucy replied adamantly, before sweeping an errant auburn lock back and smiling. "Are you going to knock, or should I?"

Chandi, looking sideways, rapped on the stout door; the old owl's familiar, "Enter," chimed from the other side. Before Chandi could announce their arrival, shouts of "Surprise!

Happy Birthday!" blared in stereo.

The look of utter awe on Chandi's face was all the confirmation Lucy needed: she had successfully surprised her roommate. Chandi stepped into the room and was immediately mobbed by well wishes. "How did you manage all this?" Chandi semi-yelled behind her.

"What, this small thing?" Lucy replied nonchalantly. Lucy was the keeper of special days, and in her book, birthdays were sacred. In the past, they were marked by small gestures: swapping undesirable chores, directing her dessert to another, or decorations made from bits of surplus materials from the monastery's production. However, this year, Lucy convinced Willem to invest some of his finder's cut from his ruin runs into a slightly bigger affair. She was able to get one of the cooks to make a small fruit and honey cake, and acquired a bottle of white lightning from a visiting tracer who had no intention of drinking it himself. When mixed with tea, herbs, and fruit juice, it was potent *and* palatable. With Brother Bartholomew's gracious offer to use his quarters, Lucy was able to invite more guests—it wasn't every day that your best friend turned seventeen. Well, technically it wasn't Chandi's birthday for another three days, but she would be on her tribute run then, and Lucy refused to let the day pass without celebration.

"Honestly, the hardest part was keeping it a secret," Lucy confessed.

Chandi took the whole scene in. The room was colorfully

decorated with lights and streamers. The organized chaos of stacked books and laboratory equipment typically found in the scholar's quarters was notably absent; in its place was a small cake with a lit candle in the middle, and a bowl of punch. Hanu and Sura were distributing drinks while Willem was in charge of keeping everyone off the cake until Chandi arrived. Her entire pathfinder training group was even there. Brother Bartholomew was stationed in his normal seat, lit pipe in hand, but the other sentients crammed into every available nook and cranny made the spacious accommodations seem otherwise cramped.

"How did you get all the pathfinders to come?" Chandi wondered aloud. Even Yan was present.

"You'd be surprised what the promise of free cake and drinks will conjure," Lucy responded snidely. "Come on. I'm not sure how much longer Willem can keep this crowd off the cake. Heaven forbid it's cut after the booze runs out."

Lucy grabbed Chandi's hand and led her to the table. Cheered on from all sides, Chandi closed her eyes, made a wish, and extinguished the flame with her breath. Somewhere amidst the din of tippled gabbing, a tune from a harmonica sang out while slices of cake made their way around the room.

"Are birthdays always like this?" Sura anxiously inquired while filling another cup.

"Oh no, this is just Lucy going above and beyond for Chandi," Hanu reassured her. "Don't worry, you've got time before Lucy realizes you've been here for over a year and haven't celebrated a birthday yet."

The reserved blonde watched the merriment from the side as she took a bite from the moist, dense cake. "I don't know… it's kinda nice having someone go through all this trouble for you, even if parties aren't your thing."

Hanu cracked a smile and merely shook his head.

Chandi went against the current in pursuit of a seat while everyone moved toward the food. She was a little overwhelmed by the hubbub. She'd never had a party just for her, as least not one that she could remember. Perhaps her parents threw her birthday parties, but she was five when she joined the church; her memory of those times was incomplete and hardly reliable. Lucy brought drinks and cake as Chandi scooted over to share her chair, which were scarce and in high demand. Chandi took a bite of her birthday cake; the spiced honey-sweetened crumb was peppered with plump raisins.

"I didn't know Finn played the harmonica," Lucy commented.

Chandi scanned the crowd. "I didn't know Yan could smile, either, but wonders never cease." Lucy snorted a little of her punch. Mira and Natalie were co-telling Joshi and Willem a story while Brother Bartholomew and Jukka seemed to be discussing the nuances of pheromone-based communication among chlorophyll-based life.

"Those two look cozy." Lucy nodded toward Hanu and

Sura.

"They do, don't they?" Chandi concurred, content in the calm they shared amidst the crowd. "You really are the best, you know? I have no idea how I'm going to match this."

Lucy grinned. "I could use some help making decorations for the next couple of weeks…" Chandi tacitly agreed and resigned herself to a month of glue and glitter. It was worth the sacrifice.

"Aren't you going to ask what I wished for?" Chandi baited her best friend.

Lucy shook her head indignantly. "Then it won't come true!" She leaned back in their shared chair. "But if you want to tell me, I'll listen. Because I'm a good friend."

As Lucy predicted, the first of the pathfinders made their excuses as soon as they had their cake, and the rest trickled out as the punch bowl ran dry. Brother Bartholomew's definition of "a small party" was clearly different than Lucy's, but the scholar knew there was little wisdom in blaming youth for being young. He kept his chair and his pipe, earned an extra slice of cake and had prudently steered clear of the punch, so things could have gone much worse. More importantly, Chandi looked genuinely happy. After the burden of being Moonstone's secret keeper, it was nice to see her in high spirits.

Once everyone was gone, Chandi joined Lucy, Hanu, and Willem in the cleanup effort, which was thankfully minimal—morning devotion waits for no one. As they were about to leave him to his pipe and peace, Brother Bartholomew beckoned Chandi to stay a little while longer. While the others headed for bed, Chandi took a seat.

"I know it's not quite your birthday, but since your party was early, I see no reason not to give you your gift a little early as well." Bartholomew produced a small, capped glass bottle from one of his inner pockets and placed it in Chandi's open palm. "It's a freshwater pearl. You simply put it in your canteen and it will create clean, fresh drinking water. Just make sure you secure the lid, or the blighter will keep making more water." From his tone, Chandi surmised his advice was from experience. "It's all the rage among the tracers and I was able to procure one for you—figured it might come in handy on long runs," he alluded obliquely.

She examined the milky pea-sized stone surrounded by water, holding it against the light. Its irregular curves revealed a soft luster as she gently shook it in its bottle. Chandi slipped it in her pocket, rose, and hurled her arms around him. "It's absolutely perfect," she mumbled into his feathers. Even with her growth and his shrinking, he was still taller than the pathfinder but not by much. He recalled the great discrepancy in their height when she first arrived at Unseen Waters, and fought the urge to pat her on the head. Chandi was no longer a child, and soon, even the Church of Parkour would have to acknowledge that.

Chapter Two

"Don't worry, you're ready," Lucy told the newest novice for the third time during breakfast.

Sura wobbled her head ambivalently. She wasn't sure why she was so nervous all of the sudden. Hadn't this been what she wanted? Her training and all those morning runs squarely led her here, so why did she suddenly feel like she wanted to puke her porridge?

Lucy nudged Willem with her elbow and gave him an unmistakable look. *Say something nice.*

Willem cleared his throat. "It's normal to feel a little nervous. After all, you only started training a few months ago..." He stopped mid-sentence once Lucy's eye daggers reached him. "You've been working so hard, I'm sure you'll be fine," he finished curtly before he could get in any more trouble.

Chandi tried a different tactic. "What's your favorite part of meditation?"

"Jumping and balance," Sura quickly answered without having to think about it.

Chandi gave her an incredulous look. She had been stuck by Dendra's nettles so many times over the years that it was difficult to fathom *that* being a runner's favorite part of meditation through movement. "Okay," Chandi quickly regained a neutral tone, "so start there your first day. Do something you like, something you're good at. You'll have to do all the stations eventually, but as a novice, you get to choose what movements you do on any given day. You aren't a tenderfoot anymore; no one's going to tell you what to do as long as you aren't slacking off or neglecting an aspect of meditation."

"Or," Hanu interjected, "you could run with Lucy or me for your first couple of days. Sometimes a friendly face is all you need." The quiet blonde gave this some thought and she managed to finish the rest of her porridge once her stomach roiled a little less.

With breakfast devoured, everyone scattered their separate ways. "You really have a way with words," Chandi observed aloud; she couldn't resist needling Willem just a bit.

"I was trying to help," Willem made his defense. "It's all fine and well to encourage her, but some sentients find it helpful when you acknowledge they have legitimate reasons to be worried. That they aren't overreacting or crazy."

"Maybe you have a point," Chandi replied diplomatically, "but there is a time and place for a dose of reality. Would you really have wanted someone to point out how many times you tried out for pathfinder trials right before your run?"

Willem winced. "Point taken," he conceded. "Between the late night and the punch, I'm not at my best this morning."

Chandi laughed. "Don't worry, our entire cohort was at the party, and they definitely had their fair share of refreshments last night."

Unlike the novices and tenderfoots who meditated through movement in the afternoon, the pathfinder trainees' mornings were dedicated to running either the adaptive training ground or the ruins of Watertown, the latter up to three to four times a week now. On a normal morning, Chandi and Willem would be heading to the locker room, but today was different. Today, they would be start their extended preceptorships.

As they entered the classroom, those already present greeted them warmly with that unspoken camaraderie between those who had shared a fond happening. Mira and Natalie motioned for Chandi to take a seat next to them, and Jukka gave Willem a subtle nod. Chandi and Willem exchanged puzzled looks and shrugs before settling in. The dynamic duo—as Chandi had taken to calling Natalie and Mira—were in the midst of complimenting her on a great party. They constituted their own call-and-response, leaving Chandi little to do but nod and smile. *Who knew having a party would bring more cachet than out-running a groue horror?* Chandi pondered rhetorically.

"Any idea who the preceptors will be?" Chandi delicately changed the subject. Natalie gave Mira a conspiratorial look, and with a nod, the pair decided to share their intel.

"Well, all we know is that they are tracers-in-training, so they are probably only a few years older than us at most," Natalie started.

"But, one of them came back to the monastery for training after running in a sept for a couple of years," Mira added furtively.

"Is that even a thing?" Chandi wondered aloud. She always though the choice was pathfinder or tracer at the end of training. While it was technically an option to join a sept as a pathfinder, the church was greatly in favor of the latter, since tracers were assets they could move from sept to sept as their special abilities were needed.

"It's an unusual path, but at least one sentient ran it," Natalie quipped. "I also heard they are short on preceptors since our cohort is so big. So maybe we'll share preceptors?"

"Or maybe use guest tracers?" Mira suggested. The mere mention of such measures caused Chandi to raise an eyebrow. Even though preceptors were always a scarce commodity, visiting tracers were rarely used as they were often called away on short notice. They mostly provided extra instructional support, where they could be useful if present but where an abrupt absence would leave neither the teaching staff nor the students in the lurch.

"All I know is there are a couple of tracers I've seen pass through here that I wouldn't mind a little one-on-one time with—" she continued lasciviously.

"Mira!" Natalie chided. "Honestly, what you must think of us, Chandi!"

Before Chandi could react or comment, Bibi's lagomorphic form passed through the doorway, her long ears twitched as she picked up the latent chatter. Behind her marched four sentients the pathfinders had only seen in passing up until now. In the lead was Aka, a hulking man standing seven feet tall with shoulders as wide as two sentients of normal size. He was so built, his muscles had muscles. All exposed surfaces of his skin, including parts of his face, were ornately tattooed with black line art. When a curious Finn had asked if he was a scritcher like Netu, Aka had merely laughed at the question; his body art was his heritage, not some bug.

Beside him was Sabin, a six-foot-tall bipedal porcupine. His cascade of black and white quills lay flat on his back under a woolen cloak. It was hard to ignore his sharp claws and teeth, even in their currently relaxed state. He bent down and made a comment to Dora, a slight figure wrapped in layers of clothing. Whatever he muttered must have been amusing, as Dora found it impossible to resist the smirk that appeared on her diapsid face. Zera, the last of the group, nudged Sabin and Dora both from behind—they were supposed to be leaders setting an example. Her stern brown eyes were just shy of overt disapproval as their jocularity calmed down.

"Settle down," Bibi called the room to attention. "As you know, the remainder of your training will be with your preceptor. We will still have didactic classes and Applied Tenets of Faith, but the bulk of your running from here on out is with your preceptor."

Her tone turned serious. "These assignments are not negotiable." Bibi paused for effect, letting the statement sink it. "We have worked hard to find preceptors that will mold you into pathfinders, and we put quite a lot of thought into the pairings. However, there are rare circumstances where a dyad is not functioning. If you feel your assignment is completely unworkable, you may bring your concerns to me."

Bibi approached the chalkboard and started writing out assignments. Her brown and gray fur had the fullness and shine of a proper winter coat, her clothing merely a formality that covered her white cottontail, which would have been conspicuously visible otherwise. She finished the last curl of her flowery but legible scrawl and knocked the chalk dust from her hands. "Find your assignments. Your preceptorship starts now."

*****

The early morning mist was all but gone as the sun warmed the air. Chandi could no longer see her breath before her as she vaulted over the broken half wall, swinging her legs to one side before finding purchase on the slanted slab of plascrete. She scurried up, using her arms to compensate for the steepness of grade before launching herself toward a railing. The cold metal was bracing to her hands as she pendulated, even through her gloves. Chandi used her legs to accentuate her swing until she could release her hold and safely clear the seven-foot gap in front of her.

Dora kept a keen watch on Chandi's progress through her section of the modified training ground. She would never admit it, but she spent quite a bit of time on the set up, throwing in obstacles to test not only ability but also judgment. On a run, a pathfinder had to balance efficiency and necessity—what impediment needed to be overcome and which should be bypassed altogether. Those were the kind of choices no monastic instructor could teach. Dora only learned that lesson herself, boots on the ground, in the school of hard knocks.

Dora made a few notes: good form, planning, and attack; excellent jumps and climbing; needs more strength training and adaptive flexibility; ambitious and hungry. *Something has lit a fire in this girl*, Dora thought to herself. The corners of her mouth rose. *I can work with that.* She jotted down a list of exercises in a training schedule. Chandi was fast, quiet, and skillful, and by the end of training, she was also going to be strong and supple.

Dora turned to Willem, her other trainee. She was pretty sure their shared amphibious heritage played a large part in his assignment, that and the fact they wanted each tracer-in-training to have experience working with male and female trainees whenever possible. He was a fine runner who made economic choices. He seemed to know his limitations and calculated that into his pathing. Dora had run with his type before—what he lacked in moxie, he made up for in reliability. He played it safe, which wasn't a bad strategy under the shattered moon. *What an odd pair I have*, Dora mused as she allowed her gaze to wander to other parts of the managed simulation zone.

Ever the consummate physical trainer, Aka had organized his section into stations, each focusing on a specific aspect of mobility. He was barking orders as Mira and Finn took turns on the footwork and quickness line. Dora was hardly surprised—half of the exercises she had planned for Chandi were things he had shown her at one time or another.

Sabin had abandoned his cloak and ran alongside Jukka and Natalie in his section of the adaptive training ground. His striped coloring blurred as he moved. Every once in a while, he would do something erratic to see how they would react. Dora couldn't help giggling as Natalie took a quill on one side and one of Jukka's thorns on the other. *Leave it to Sabin to make himself the obstacle.*

And then there was Zera, the youngest tracer-in-training and quite possibly the most sober sentient Dora had ever met. There wasn't anything wrong with Zera per se, just that she took everything—including herself—so damn seriously. One would be tempted to chalk it up to her age; when you aren't much older than your trainees, it's tempting to put some distance between yourself and them. However, Zera had always been that way, even as a novice—wound as tight as a screw. If there was a test, she needed to score the highest. If there was a rule, she needed to make sure she followed it to the letter. If there was doubt, she needed to squash it. Zera lived in a black and white world; there was no place for gray.

Dora's attention lastly fell on Joshi and Yan, Zera's students. The first was utterly bored and the second was rapt with attention, zeroed in on Zera's deep-set eyes and hanging on her every word. *Oh dear*, Dora thought, *have we found someone to out-Zera Zera?* Dora wrapped herself a little tighter in her clothes at the thought and called her pathfinders in for a regroup and huddle.

Chapter Three

Khiri's robes billowed slightly as she paced the hallways with her prioress; the Monastery of Unseen Water's abbess preferred to be on the move whenever possible. The tigress held her hands behind her back and listened attentively while Ariadne reviewed the monastery's projects: recently completed, currently ongoing, and prospectively slotted. The arachnid administrator juggled a litany of checklists in her multiple arms while the click of her remaining chitinous limbs kept time like a living metronome.

The flooded root cellar had been dried and sealed, just in time to store this year's harvest. This year had a bumper crop in the orchards with a projected twenty-five percent increase in cider production over last year—Ariadne was already working on procuring more barrels. The gristmill repairs seemed to be holding, but she had added it to list of things for the tinker to look over when he visited next week. Winterization plans were underway with each department tasked to compile a list of necessary and desired repairs to maximize the monastery's resources and time.

As Ariadne started going over the numbers, Khiri's mind began to wander. The tigress had already reviewed the paperwork after breakfast, but she allowed the prioress—who thrived on routine—to continue her summation. The long and short of it was that Unseen Waters was sound, but stockpiling food and materials in anticipation of supply disruptions caused by King Dexter VI's most recent war surge.

Khiri had spent the past decade plus insinuating herself into their benefactor's domestic retinue as Chandi's guardian during her monthly tribute trips. As much as the tigress hated to admit it, things were not going well in the Kingdom of a Thousand Islands and it was her job to shield the monastery as much as possible from the vagaries of war. And then there was the matter of how much longer the visits would continue. Once Chandi turned seventeen, the agreement made between her parents and the Church of Parkour would no longer be valid. The decision to continue her service to the church in that capacity would be hers alone to make, and Khiri did not relish having to have that conversation with the promising runner.

As they strolled down a passage lined with windows, the abbess caught her reflection in the glass. As she neared the image, the distortion lessened until she could almost recognize the countenance that started back at her. Ariadne's voice cut through her contemplation. "Abbess?" Khiri halted her stride and looked for the prioress, who had stopped moments earlier. "Are you feeling quite well? You have a queer look on your face." Khiri gave a reassuring nod and motioned for her to proceed.

*****

When Chandi received Khiri's summons at the end of Applied Tenets of Faith, she asked for clarification twice, just to be certain she didn't misunderstand the missive: late afternoon chores in the southern garden? The gardens were all but picked and most of the labor had moved on to other facets of harvest and preservation. Typically, the abbess called upon students to visit her in the privacy of her office, and the last time Chandi met Khiri outside that familiar venue, she became the keeper of Moonstone. The recollection sent a shiver down her spine, despite the warmth of her body from working the mats and the layers of outer garments she'd donned for the falling temperatures of late afternoon. Chandi was confused and a bit worried, but a summons was a summons, so she made her way to the southern garden to find Khiri busy digging up turnips.

Chandi's soft steps sank into the overturned soil as she worked her way toward the kneeling tigress. Khiri unearthed another turnip from the ground, fastidiously brushing off the large clumps of dirt from the bulb before adding it to the basket. The abbess adhered to the notion that everyone contributed to Unseen Waters' upkeep, and unlike many of its inhabitants, she found chores to be one of her favorite times of the day. There was a clarity of purpose that allowed the mind to still while one worked—it was as close as the abbess got to running these days. She found time slowed and nebulous situations came into focus after a few hours of honest manual labor.

Chandi found it oddly reassuring that such an otherwise imposing figure gave such care to a simple turnip. As stealthy as her steps were, they were no match for the abbess's keen ears. "Sister of the stride, do you intend to stand there and watch, or help? These turnips are not going to dig themselves up and the root cellar is finally ready to receive them."

Adequately chastised, Chandi let out a quiet, "Yes, Abbess," before kneeling beside her. The soil was moist and packed from recent rains, making extraction more difficult than normal, but it had to be done before the winter crops could be sown. One by one, the basket filled as hands moved through the dirt.

"Your birthday is coming in a few days," Khiri broke the silence. Out of the corner of her eye, she watched Chandi nod without stopping her harvest. "Seventeen, if the records are correct."

"That is my understanding, Abbess," Chandi responded. The pathfinder wasn't entirely sure where the conversation was headed, but it felt like a trap. *Is this about the party?* she wondered, keeping her hands busy and her face still. *Brother Bartholomew wouldn't have allowed it if it was going to get anyone in trouble.* She felt Khiri's hand rest on her arm and still her labor.

"We need to discuss your future with the Church of Parkour," the abbess began. Chandi's heart skipped a beat. Khiri rolled off her knees and onto her heels, knocking the dirt off her hands. Crouched down, the discrepancy in their heights was lessened, allowing them to speak face-to-face.

She continued, "When you first came to the monastery, it was under an agreement between your parents and the church. Your parents were quiet adamant that certain provisions should be in place before they would agree to relinquish you." Chandi's stomach churned; this was the first time anyone in the church made reference to her life before the faith, however brief that was, much less mention her parents directly.

"First, they wanted to ensure that you had a proper education and the opportunity to train." Chandi blinked twice rapidly. "Second, they wanted the choice to remain in service with the church to be yours when you came of age…" Khiri paused. "When you turned seventeen." The abbess watched the news percolate through the pathfinder's racing mind.

Chandi raised her earnest green eyes from the ground. "What does all this mean?" she barely spoke above a whisper.

"It means, once you turn seventeen, you can decide if you want to continue service to the church," Khiri clarified. "We will perform the upcoming tribute to the king's estate since your birthday falls during that visit, but if you wish, that could be your last tribute visit on behalf of the Church of Parkour." Khiri could almost see the gears churning and held her tongue, waiting for a barrage of questions.

"If I don't go on tribute visits, would I still get to train?" Chandi cautiously inquired.

"Given your talent and progress, I don't foresee that being a problem," Khiri answered diplomatically.

"What happens to my parents and my village if I don't go on tribute trips anymore?"

"The old agreements would be null and void. They would retain any physical improvements the church has already installed, but future investments and protections would cease." The abbess watched the line of Chandi's face shift back and forth as she clinched and relaxed her jaw.

"And if I agree to keep going?"

"Then you can choose to renew the terms of the existing agreement or renegotiate different terms, if you would prefer," Khiri subtly volunteered.

"Different terms?" Chandi voiced in puzzled awe.

"Certainly. Your parents agreed to your service to the Kingdom of a Thousand Islands because their village was in its domain, but you could offer different parameters to your service: specify duration, frequency, or location of service. The worse the church can say is 'no.'"

Chandi set her gaze to the northeast in the general direction of her village, her back toward the setting sun. "Could I return?"

"Yes, if you wanted to sever all ties, including training, with the Church of Parkour, you could return to your village,"

Khiri affirmed uncomfortably. "But you would have to travel under your own auspices. Once you break with the church, your safety is no longer their concern." The cool breeze stung Chandi's eyes and further reddened her cheeks. She had been on the inside for so long, she had forgotten the harsh reality of life beneath the shattered moon. She turned her face back to the abbess.

"How long do I have to think about it?"

"Nothing has to be decided right away, but I can't stall the issue indefinitely. The church will want resolution one way or another by the end of year. If you know what you would like to do, we can start preparations." Khiri reached out and softened her tone. "And if you have questions…"

Chandi reflexively flinched at her approach but nodded. "I'm sure I will later, but this is about all I can handle at the moment." She stood and grabbed on side of the nearly full basket. "We should get these turnips inside."

*****

Cassie closed the folio and leaned back in her chair. She knew being the otherworld advisor for the elder council was not for the faint of heart, she just didn't anticipate the degree to which some days would be this trying. She rolled with the punches when the deadline for next year's budget was pushed up. She muscled through when her committee meeting ran long.

She didn't even snap at Councilman Kolas for eviscerating her proposal during said meeting—even though he was privately in favor of it—because "it wouldn't look good for someone in my position to support a measure put forth by someone of your disposition." Cassie couldn't be sure what he meant by the comment: was it because she was a sorcerer? Human? Female? Not an ancient fundamentalist wackadoodle in love with stroking their own ego through the thinly disguised language of the faith?

She closed her eyes and rubbed her temples with the tips of her fingers. The sorcerer was so focused on staving off the incipient headache that she didn't even hear the knock on the door before it opened.

"You look like a woman who could use some good news. And maybe a drink?"

Cassie opened her eyes and spied a friendly face and an even friendlier bottle of wine. "Leo, I could kiss you if you weren't part cactus." She motioned for him to close the door behind him.

"Some sentients like the pain," Leo quipped cheekily, producing two glasses tucked into various pockets.

Cassie grinned. "Shut up and pour." She swirled the pink liquid in her glass. She wasn't normally a rosé kind of girl, but this was a nice bottle, if a little on the sweet side. "So what's the good news?"

Leo crossed his legs and made a production of sipping

his wine. Cassie knew it had to be something big for him to pause for dramatic impact. "The lab minions finished the containment box."

Cassie almost spat out her wine. "What?! But that's two months ahead of schedule. The lab swore up and down that six months was the fastest turnaround time."

Leo leaned in. "Apparently, someone brought in a rare ultra spirit that wasn't slated for any other object." He slammed his hand down on her desk for emphasis.

Cassie's eyes narrowed. "This wouldn't have anything to do with the fact that the octopoids received our most recent envoy and have asked for help with their spirit problem in Oswego?"

"I have no idea what you are talking about—I'm not privy to that level of council knowledge," he answered coyly. A full-throttle laugh left Cassie's belly; if she hadn't known him so well, she would have believed him. "You know, you should do that more often," Leo suggested. "I was worried your facial muscles had forgotten how to smile."

Cassie regained her composure and her glass. "So who was it? Councilman Luther? Councilwoman Dunn?"

Leo shrugged his shoulders. "I honestly don't know who approved the resources, but it appears you have at least one friend in high places that is fine with expediting the inevitable. Take the win!"

Cassie harrumphed. "It's not the favors I take objection to, it's their price."

"If they don't call in the marker, it costs nothing…"

Cassie handed her glass to Leo for a refill. "What color is the sky in your world? Is the moon still broken there?" She felt the vibration of his baritone laugh through the glass.

"I guess the question is, are you going on the road or staying here with these stacks of papers?"

Cassie drained her second glass. "I'll pack my case."

Chapter Four

Chandi tossed and turned in bed to the sound of Lucy's deep breathing—bordering a light snore—in the bunk above her. There was little hope for sleep after her discussion with the abbess. She wasn't sure how she felt about any of it and proceeded to try different moods like one tries on hats, to see which seemed to fit and flatter. First, she was angry—*why didn't anyone tell me all this before? How much time have I spent in fear of not being allowed to run?*

Then she flirted with paranoia—*the abbess must have known the whole time. Who else knew and didn't tell me? Did Brother Bartholomew know? He couldn't; he would have told me. Surely, he would have told me.* Which was only a short leap to disillusion. Her whole life, she'd adhered to the sentiment that she went where she was needed without ever questioning who was making that determination. *It certainly wasn't me*, she thought bitterly.

Before long, Chandi felt simultaneously trapped and guilty—*I don't really have a choice. I have to keep serving. If I stop using my abilities to fulfill tribute, my family will lose their benefits. However, if I left altogether, at least I could help them more directly. But then I would have to leave.* Chandi's heart sank. Even though it felt like a betrayal to her parents, Unseen Waters had become home and she had become a runner.

As much as feeling bad could feel good, the momentary catharsis passed as she tumbling down dark thoughts and darker emotions. After hours of exhausting rumination, Chandi was covering the same ground as before and she had to admit that none of this brought her answers or solace. Reluctantly, she closed her eyes. Amidst the turmoil in her mind, she formed a small bubble of stillness and slowly inflated it, pushing back on the turbulence until there was only the tranquility of nothingness.

Unfortunately, the next morning greeted her with the same dilemma: *what do I do?* Chandi found herself once again—possibly for the last time—in a Church of Parkour carriage headed out for tribute. The clip of the horses' hooves was interrupted only by the snap of the banner waving in the cold wind. The inside had been fitted with traveling rugs to make the journey more comfortable, and the heavy curtains significantly cut out the draft at the expense of light and the view. Chandi considered how many times she had ridden this road: one hundred forty. She'd done the math last night.

Chandi felt the indirect gaze of the abbess sitting across from her. She knew she was being observed, which prompted an instinctive urge to be unseen. The pathfinder pulled back on the curtain, letting the crisp clean air in as she took a peek at the passing scenery. There were no recent battles out this way, yet the landscape still bore signs of the war: fields were stripped bare and everything was lean. When there was an army to feed, the countryside went hungry. Chandi spied something in the road ahead just as one of the guards in front passed word to the guard within the carriage: obstruction ahead.

An agglomeration of scrap wood, metal, and found material stood in the middle of the road, and although it was generous to call it a wagon, the missing wheel that caused it to list to one corner lent it credibility. The wind died down as the carriage slowed to a stop. The rear guard advanced to the front to assess the situation—thirty minutes to clear the way using the horses. As the guards started to unyoke the front two horses from the church's carriage, the sisters of the stride heard the guards in front ready their weapons.

Chandi didn't recognize the piercing staccato as gunfire at first, but when the guard pulled Chandi away from the window and down to the floor of carriage where Khiri had instinctively stooped, she quickly grasped the situation: they were under attack. Her ears rang as the Order of the Guard returned fire, the closest mere inches from her. The horses reared at the sound of shots, jerking the carriage and jostling its inhabitants. The driver quickly steadied the horses and as the world tumbled outside, Chandi curled into a ball, shutting out the chaos.

Only when she felt Khiri's hand on her back did Chandi

dare to open her eyes and pull her hands from her ears. Khiri motioned for silence; the acrid smell of spent gunpowder and the cries of the wounded were all that lingered. The guard who had pulled Chandi to safety moments earlier was unconscious but he was still breathing and there was no apparent blood oozing out of him. Khiri signed to Chandi: *No matter what happens, stay hidden.* The stunned pathfinder nodded and watched the tigress glide out of the carriage door.

Khiri channeled her adrenaline into hypervigilant assessment as she slinked into the deepest of shadows. The firefight was all but over with no apparent fatalities among the Order of the Guard who had taken effective defensive positions against their would-be hijackers. By the distribution of their dead attackers, it looked as if they had been going after the horses and carriage. Without success, the abbess grimly noted.

She sniffed the air and smelt blood and, from father away, fear. A scan of the nearby landscape revealed a few rocky outcroppings, broken masonry, and defoliated trees in which to take cover, but the glint of metal in sparse sunlight gave away the location of what remained of the failed bandits. As fearful as the duo smelled, she knew their desperation must be greater, for only the desperate would attack a carriage under the church's flag. Khiri chose a regrettable but required course of action and summoned her stillness—desperation and fear are a dangerous combination, especially when armed.

New shots were fired as Khiri leapt from the shadows, but

none found their mark as she arced her body through the air with feline agility, springing off the ground and tacking off a rocky surface to land behind the remains of a wall. The Order of the Guard provided aggressive cover—none wanted to imagine what their captain would say if the abbess was injured on their watch.

From the shadows behind the wall, Khiri's constricted pupils zeroed in. Another bounding leap and she was in the midst of her prey, who quivered in the presence of the seven-foot tigress. With a swift blow, she disarmed one assailant and knocked the other off balance with a well-timed crouch and extended leg. A twist of her razor-sharp rear claws slashed through soft flesh while her teeth tore through gushing veins until there were no more death cries, and silence once again settled over the dreary cold land.

There may be no stillness in violence, but there was undeniably something there: primal instinct. Khiri licked the blood off her hands and face, but there was little that could be done about her bloodied clothes, at least until they arrived at the king's estate. She took a deep breath and tucked away her predatory predilections where she carefully cradled them; she was once more the mother of the stride. She gave the all-clear before venturing out from behind the wall, reassuring the Order of the Guard that the blood on her clothing was not her own.

No one made mention of the abbess's appearance as she

entered the carriage to rejoin the company of her ward and the now-conscious guard within. The remaining soldiers got to work, clearing the road and hustling to their destination before any more trouble could find them.

The rest of the journey passed in tense silence, but none could stave off the ruckus of royal indignation once the condition of their travel became known to His Royal Highness, King Dexter Albert Winchester VI, ruler of the Kingdom of a Thousand Islands. "This is an outrage!" echoed through the halls of his estate before petering out to pacing and yells from his study.

Home after a successful campaign with the Oswald brothers in the southeast, Dexter was ambivalent about returning home for the winter. On one hand, he wasn't as young as he used to be, and a warm fire, soft bed, and hearty meals with a nice claret never sounded as nice as it had this season. However, once home, the inactivity gnawed on him. The estate didn't require his presence to function, a testament to his capable staff but just another annoyance to the restless monarch. But this incursion gave him somewhere to focus his pent-up energy. He shook with equal parts rage and delight; he had an enemy to root out.

As the king enjoyed a good fury, the rest of his estate tended to the pressing matters at hand. Injuries were dressed, arrangements were made for more security on their return in two days' time, and Khiri—who never brought extra clothing for the short trip—was found suitable attire while hers was washed. Luckily for the abbess, the king's estate knew how to deftly remove blood and gore from clothing after years of their bellicose lord's warring. While there was little hope of finding anything to fit a seven-foot-tall bipedal tigress, with a little creativity, Khiri found herself covered in an ensemble of draped cloth, strategically secured with pins and stitches.

As for Chandi, Chef Pasleur swooped in, wrapped her in a blanket, and stuffed her with hot liquids and food. Tucked away in a cozy corner of the kitchen, the bustle and warmth lulled the exhausted pathfinder to sleep. Both Khiri and Claudette agreed to let her rest, and the mother of the stride cradled her ward in her arms and carried her to bed while the cook set aside a tray for when she woke, inevitably hungry.

*****

Khiri flipped the loose end of cloth over her left shoulder before starting her soup. While she was grateful that one of the maids was able to concoct a garment for her, she was unaccustomed to clothing that required fussing. Her practical vestments and robes kept her warm and covered without inhibiting her movement; the same could not be said of her current attire. But she made an effort as his royal highness was entertaining tonight.

Seated to his left was his only surviving child and to his

right, her husband and his son-in-law. Khiri hadn't seen much of Amelia since her marriage two years ago—only once at her mother's funeral. Her curly mop was now tamed into a tidy coiffed braided crown her skinned knees and muddy hands were now bedecked in layers of fine silks and velvets and jewels, and her stomach was noticeably swollen. Khiri might not have recognized her were it not for her eyes; there remained a shrewd glint behind the blue sparkle belying an astute mind behind her bubbly speech and dimples.

Emma, as her close intimates and those that knew her from her youth called her, was telling the abbess how disappointed she was that Chandi was not at dinner, but completely understood given the circumstances. Waylaid by bandits—she couldn't even imagine! Then she talked about the lovely manor Stephen had built for them with the new baby on the way, although she wouldn't hear about actually having the baby there. She insisted that she should return home to have her first child. Even though her mother was no longer alive, it was only right to give birth where she was born. She felt like her mother's spirit would watch over her. "Does that sound silly?" The princess clearly posed the question rhetorically as she barely took a breath before rattling off possible baby names. Khiri nodded politely, keeping a keen ear fixed to the discussion happening across the table.

Dexter grinned at his daughter's effortless gayety; when she smiled, she looked so much like her mother, although not as much as when she was cross. Thankfully, she was buoyant by nature. His eye was drawn to the abbess seated beside his daughter, inconspicuously adjusting her wrap to keep it from landing on her roast. He was so used to her plain, dowdy dress that it was startling to discover that the mother of the stride had breasts under all that wool. The Church of Parkour sigil ensorcelled on her arm became partially visible each time her wrap slipped past her shapely shoulders. Dexter came to his senses once he realized his son-in-law was waiting for an answer to a question he didn't hear.

"What was that, my boy?"

"I was making a suggestion about troop allocation for the spring offensive," Stephen redirected his father-in-law, who had a habit of drinking too much in the gloom of winter.

"Papa, no talking business at the family dinner table!" Emma quickly reminded him of the long-standing rule her mother had established.

"Who's talking business?" Dexter rebutted with forced levity. "I was just congratulating your husband on his fine work brokering peace with the Ontario League earlier this year." He shot Stephen a look. He knew all too well his daughter's temper could turn on a dime. Add to that the vagaries of pregnancy....

"That's right, darling. He was just saying what a fine statesman I was turning into," Stephen corroborated Dexter's cover of his indiscretion.

Emma's glare softened. "Well then, I guess that's okay."

Adequately pacified, she proceeded to talk all about the strange habits in the Ontario League she had learned from Stephen. "Do you know they eat tree sap? Love the stuff!"

As dinner wound down, Emma retreated to her room for a rest. Khiri was exhausted just listening to Emma's stream of consciousness and was about to make her excuses when Dexter called to her. "Abbess, would you be so kind as to stop by my study before you retire? I wonder if it would be possible for you to pinpoint where the attack on your carriage occurred to better inform my response. Unless you aren't overly tired...." Dexter let the invitation linger.

"As you wish, your highness," she replied with a formal bow. She held the front of her makeshift dress down to maintain modesty, but that didn't stop it from gathering around her hips. The mother of the stride left the men to their brandy and cigars. As she walked away, Dexter could almost make out the swish of her tail under the shifting fabric.

Chapter Five

The small room was sparsely furnished—just a chair and a table. The lit candle flickered shadows of the cups sitting on the table upon the wall. Chandi wasn't to drink from them, just sit next to them—that's what the brother of the stride told her before he hastily left the room. She stared at the closed door, already bored with the exercise; they could have at least let her bring a book.

Her legs dangled in the air, not quite long enough to reach the floor. She sang herself a song her mother had taught her about a girl wandering the forest, unaware of the dangers lurking in the shadows but guarded by faithful gods and goddesses watching over her. The singing helped with the tummy ache she always got when she first entered the room. It got better as time passed and the initial nausea lessened to a mild distress, not unlike when she was hungry. It had started with just one cup, but more would be on the table the next time she entered. She was up to ten.

Chandi stopped her song; she heard a trickle. Her twin braids ricocheted as she turned her head—the water was overflowing the cups' rims at an alarming speed. The table was already covered in a thin watery veneer with puddles forming in the low spots of the uneven floor. Chandi ran to the door and pulled—it was locked. She banged on the door; the water was already to her knees.

She looked at the cups. She wasn't supposed to drink the water, but she couldn't think of anything else to do. She picked up the first and drank deeply, but no matter how much she swallowed, the vessel never emptied. She tried a second and a third, but the result was the same. The water was now waist-high.

Chandi opened her mouth to scream, but all that came out was more water, filling the room even faster. She swam to the door and beat her body against it. As she grasped for the handle again, she felt something grab her arms and then her legs. She struggled against the unseen restraints as the water snuffed out the candle. She was underwater now and she could feel her limbs being pulled outward, like she was being torn asunder. She could feel herself succumbing, sinking in a cell of water.

That was when Chandi woke, startled and actually relieved to hear her own screams. She took stock of her surroundings, eventually piecing together where she was. The door flew open. "Are you all right?" The abbess scanned the room for immediate threats.

"Yes, Abbess. It was just a bad dream," Chandi reassured the taut mother of the stride. Khiri flagged the other members of the household that all was fine, crossed the threshold, and closed the door behind her.

She lit the lamp on the table and motioned toward the covered plate. "Are you hungry? Chef Pasleur made you a tray."

Chandi marveled at the abbess's outfit but hid her awe quickly. "Not right now," Chandi tersely replied.

Khiri put her foot down. "You haven't eaten in hours; try to eat a little something. I think Chef even made you a little treat for your birthday." Khiri unveiled cuts of roast with slices of bread, stewed fruit, and a little marzipan pig. The tigress picked up the porcine treat. "She must have saved up her sugar a while to make this gem. It's almost too pretty to eat." She deposited it into Chandi's lap.

The pathfinder examined the decoration and declared, "Almost," as she bit into the confection. The sweet smooth almond paste coated her mouth. Just then, Chandi realized how hungry she was and accepted the tray, tearing into her food. She saved the rest of the little pig for later.

The stiff tension between them lessened for a moment, and Khiri seized her chance. She took a seat beside Chandi's feet, giving her plenty of space. "Chandi, I want you to know that I made your parents a promise to watch after you in their place. Your parents trusted me all those years ago, and I hope you feel like you can trust me, too. I'm not the enemy."

"Why didn't you tell me sooner?" Her voice was small but raw.

The abbess opened her hands in gesture. "There was nothing to tell until the time came."

"Do you know much I worried about not being allowed to train?" Chandi's tone bore more incrimination that she had realized. The abbess looked wounded and honestly confused.

"Did anyone from the church give you the impression that you would *not* be allowed to train?"

"Not exactly…"

"It would seem counterproductive to bring you to a training monastery and not let you run," Khiri pointed out as neutrally as possible. A rising blush rose to Chandi's cheeks; she felt foolish and childish. Where had she gotten the idea? Had she really fabricated the anxiety out of nothing?

The abbess wanted to comfort her while simultaneously shaking some sense into her. "If you had come to me with your fears, I would have told you sooner. I'm sorry it weighed so heavy on you. That was never my intention." The pathfinder gave a small but appreciable nod. Khiri could live with that. "You should try to get some rest after you eat." Khiri rose and left the lamp lit for Chandi. "You'll have a full day ahead of you tomorrow. Emma is home."

*****

Chandi had tried to slip out of the house unnoticed, but Emma was on her like a hawk. Apparently, there wasn't much hope for a full night's sleep at this late stage of her pregnancy. She looked like a python that had just fed—normal arms, normal torso, and then *bam*! Emma looked so miserable propped up on pillows on the chaise lounge, Chandi didn't have to heart of say no to tea after her perambulation.

Chandi never made it to the library last night, so she didn't have any books with her as she walked the estate, just her thoughts. The past muddied the present, and Chandi found herself growing sentimental at every sight. When she made a stop at the barn, she sighed at the sight of Bessie, her favorite cow, because this could be the last night she got to pet her. When she walked past the well, she thought about all the ancient coins she and Emma had dropped down the well and where all those wishes had gone. As she passed the neglected gardens and hedge maze, she became nostalgic for those summer days when she and Emma would run the maze while her mother clipped flowers.

Friendship is a nebulous thing; it took so many forms that calling it all the same name seemed disingenuous. On the surface, one could regard Emma and Chandi as friends. They were roughly the same age, spent a great deal of time together growing up, and were present for some of life's big milestones—well, at least Emma's. Minimally speaking, it was a friendship of proximity and circumstance. It's not like there were very many children a princess could play with when her mother was fiercely protective and her father was at war with all of their neighbors.

For a while, Chandi thought she was special because she got to see the real Emma, not the living doll she deigned to be in order to keep the peace in the Winchester home. The Emma she knew loved to read just as much as Chandi. She gladly traded her frocks for trousers and ran over the estate with Chandi on her monthly visits. She was a willing co-conspirator when it came to sneaking sweets from the kitchen.

But that all changed when Emma "became a young lady" as her mother put it. Suddenly, the other Emma took over—the Emma that cared about her complexion and figure, who didn't want to get her dress dirty, soothed with her dimples, and "simply couldn't fathom!" The Emma that constantly wondered "what would *they* think?" and never had a satisfactory answer when Chandi dared to ask who "they" were. Every once in a while, Chandi thought she caught a glimpse of the old Emma, but it was like seeing a shadow—it was fleeting and you could only catch it when the light was just so.

Chef Pasleur had everything set up in the blue room, the late queen's favorite lounge. Dexter had it closed when his wife died, but Emma was immediately drawn there on her return. In her mind, occupying the same space her mother once did was the closest proximity she could get to the deceased woman. With an adamant word, the cobwebs were cleared, the windows cleaned, and the furniture uncovered.

Chandi took a seat opposite Emma, who poured tea

and doled out lumps of sugar and splashes of milk. She still remembered how Chandi took her tea.

"How are you after yesterday's ordeal?" Emma asked sympathetically.

"You know me, I bounce back quickly," Chandi replied off-handedly as she loaded an array of small bites onto her plate.

"I suppose you have to be, running all those ruins. I simply couldn't fathom!" Emma shuddered at the thought.

"What about you?" Chandi changed the subject. "Married and expecting a baby—that's got to be exciting."

"Oh, you know, it's been busy, busy, busy! Stephen does a lot of traveling for papa, but he's built a fine manor for us once the baby's born. I barely finished picking the decor before we came here. You'd be amazing at how many shades of yellow there are. And you have to have an opinion. You can't say 'I don't care, as long as it's yellow'!" Emma nervously laughed. "Sorry, it's this pregnancy. It's a circus in here and I'm never really sure what is going to come out some days." Her face held its smile even as the mirth left her eyes.

Chandi wasn't sure how to answer, but something sad lingered behind Emma's twinkling blues. Chandi wanted to tell her it was going to be all right, but she couldn't be certain of that and false hope wasn't what friends give each other. "Remember when we snuck out to the village when a traveling circus was visiting?" Chandi mused about happier times. "We ate so much candy that we got sick on the seesaw. Your mom was furious and your dad just laughed."

A genuine smile spread on Emma's face. "There were juggling dwarves and a clown that told terrible jokes and sprayed us with water," she recalled.

"Yes!" Chandi exclaimed. "How could I forget about the dwarves? They were terrible jugglers—kept dropping things left and right. The crowd tossed the fruit they dropped back at them."

Emma giggled and sighed. "Things were simpler then."

Chandi nodded, lost in her own quandary. "You can say that again."

"Chandi, I'm scared," Emma blurted out. Once the facade broke and the words started slipping out, she couldn't stop them. "I don't know what I'm doing. I thought coming here would help, but now I'm not so sure. What do I know about being married or having babies? And it's not like papa or Stephen know anything about such things. I wish my mom were here. She'd know what to do."

Chandi offered Emma a comforting hand and wrestled with what to say next. Platitudes would be easy, but a measured dose of reality might actually get through to the old Emma in this candid moment. "Your mom was a force of nature," Chandi started, hedging her bets and gauging Emma's receptiveness. "No other woman could have wrangled your father under control." Emma let out a short laugh.

Screw it, the worse she can do is throw me out and this could be my last tribute visit anyway, Chandi thought to herself. "She was great at shaping your life into what she thought was best, but she never really saw you for who you are. She was too busy trying to mold you into what she wanted you to be—in her image. But you have your own life now and you're starting your own family. I may know nothing about all that, but I think it would be a shame to let the specter of your mother dictate how your marriage and family should be."

They were very still and silent for some time; Chandi didn't want to risk upsetting the calm. "Umph—the baby is kicking up a storm," Emma spoke at last. "You wanna feel?" Before she could answer, the princess placed Chandi's hand on the underside of her bulging belly. Chandi felt an unmistakable jab through Emma's clothing and impulsively smiled at the life within.

*****

The first snows had fallen in the ruins of Ottawa, giving each step a thick crunch under the myriad of strides. They had done well when the Ontario League was battling the Kingdom of a Thousand Islands, essentially giving them dominion over the urban remains while the two rulers vied for more space amid the shifting borders of war. And then President de Frontenac came to leadership, unifying the otherwise fractured communities of Ontario. Under his banner, they gained ground and successfully sued for peace.

Little could they have anticipated that Ontario's reconciliation with Dexter VI was the beginning of their troubles. Emboldened by their gains, the sorcerous President de Frontenac called for taking back Ottawa from "the muties," making alliances with the local chapter of the Church of Parkour whose runners delved deeper into the rubble with each passing moon.

There was division among them. Some wanted to stay and repel the League and the church; this ruin had become theirs and they were willing to fight for it. Others wanted to leave and blamed their recent losses on the softness that comes from staying in one place too long. They were not community builders; they were ruin dwellers. Their sentiment was if President de Frontenac wanted Ottawa, let him have it. Let them take the bounty they had already found, and march to the south to pluck riches from new ground.

As custom demanded, there was a contest of strength, both bloody and brutal. Ultimately, Terem yielded and the will of the strong prevailed. That was the rule of the ruins; that was their way. They were the inheritors of the world left beneath the shattered moon—strong enough to take what they wanted, tough enough to endure its trials. They were the Laughter at the End of Time.

Chapter Six

His Tentacled Majesty Droxithal Purammon found the girdle of power particularly heavy that cold late autumn morning. Many decades had he ruled the Lordship of Fingers, and the octopoids flourished under his leadership: the expansion from the Finger Lakes early in his reign, the creation of the militia spawned in the breeding chambers of Lake Ontario, and the economic success of the freshwater pearls as a valued trade good among the vertebrates.

Despite his successes, he wished for more. More feats. More vigor. More life. But even as he readied himself for the day, he could feel the call of his hectocotylus growing stronger with each passing day. His era was drawing to a close and it was only a matter of time. Soon, he would mate and die, and from his senescence, another generation of octopoids would bloom. The rituals must be observed and the girdle of power would be fastened around the next tentacled majesty, may his three hearts beat true.

He would have liked to witness the rise of Atlantis in his time, but so was the wish of all octopoids that preceded him and all that would come after him until the seas rose to reclaim the world. Now his hopes rested on his successor, Halldix Kepoi, fruit of his cousin's loins and finest of his brood. It was his tinkering that modified a breeding chamber into the mother-of-pearl, producing the sought-after freshwater pearls. It was his curiosity in the vertebrates that led to the discovery of humans and their capability of sensing sorcery under the shattered moon. Droxithal had no doubt about Halldix's insatiable drive for discovery nor his popularity among the other five great noble families. None would contest his regency until one of Droxithal's brood matured, but would he be ready to rule?

It was Halldix's idea to receive the Church of Parkour's emissary; the octopoids' rudimentary sorcerers could only identify the disturbance as otherworldly in nature, and vanquishing them was beyond their ability. Had he been younger, King Droxithal would have fought him on the notion and called it unoctopoid. However, times were changing, and as the calls from outside Oswego grew more frequent and frantic, His Tentacled Majesty could no longer afford to dismiss the problem or any possible means of resolution.

He took one last look in the mirror before allowing his entourage into his quarters; one last moment of quiet contemplation before the whirlwind began. He stood proudly on his two legs while his six arms gathered his hump and fastened the girdle of power just beneath. He was still the

Tentacled Majesty of the Lordship of Fingers and his three hearts remained true.

*****

The cold breeze blowing from the north abruptly stopped; a wave of spine-chilling fear spread through the Order of the Guard at this newfound quiet. Cassie raised up one hand and motioned for a perimeter. The soldiers circled the sorcerer, spears and shields ready. She reached into a pocket under the folds of her cloak and sprinkled ash in a circle as she chanted to the otherworld. She demanded their compliance, that the spirit show itself. The ash sparkled as if ignited in midair, coalescing into a winged vaguely humanoid form. As Cassie ripped it across the veil, the creature cried out, exposed to the stark cold beneath the shattered moon. Its piercing bulbous black eyes scanned its surroundings as it unfurled its wings to their full expanse, exposing four long limbs tipped with talons. It let out a screech and two of the soldiers dropped to the ground at the hideous sound, blood dripping from their ears.

The multitude of voices whispered frantically to Cassie, all vying for her attention. She pushed them to the periphery of her mind and focused on her spell. An unnatural wind blew as she recited her incantation. Black spectral bands lashed around the spirit-made-flesh and looped around again and again until its wings were crushed against its body, trussed like a spider's next meal. The creature writhed against its bonds, which emitted a crimson glow in the half-light of the cloudy sky.

The remaining soldiers closed with their stabbing spears, adrenaline coursing through their veins to stave off the terror. As the creature's vital fluids spilled out on the ground, Cassie pulled out a pendent from under her clothing: a charm warding off the evil eye. The lapis lazuli at its center was set in silvery scrollwork that gleamed from constant care and polish. As the pitiful creature drew its last breath, the sorcerer raised her voice once more and spoke in a tongue that only she and the creature could understand, "Yield and find peace."

The ebony bands contracted, twisting the creature within into oblivion. The whole of it torpedoed into Cassie's pendent, piercing the charm in its perfectly round blue eye. The Order of the Guard stood down once the cold wind resumed from the north, helping their fallen comrades-in-arms find their feet, and Cassie breathed a sigh of relief.

It had been a rough week in the ruins of Oswego, hunting spirits during the day and searching for Moonstone in secret at night. Cassie came loaded for bear—she didn't know what kind of spirits had crossed over through the lunar meteorite, not to mention the typical dangers of the ruins, which were wild and untouched. As a general rule, the octopoids had little interest in ruins, but when the spirits started to encroach on their nearby settlements, they could no longer ignore the crumbling remnants of the ancients.

The Church of Parkour knew how to survive in such environs and placed their tents just on the ruins' edge, granting them unprecedented access to Oswego as the mutated fresh water octopoids stayed within their encampments. They watched the vertebrates with equal parts suspicion and curiosity; everything thing about them seemed foreign: their clothing, their food, their movement, their inadequate number of arms.

Lord Halldix oversaw the octopoid militia and greeted the Church of Parkour on their arrival. His stately demeanor was polite and perfunctory despite his common field attire. He left the church to their work during the day but invited the sorcerer to dine with him in the evenings "to exchange ideas of their different cultures." Cassie obliged in spite of her reservations—as if Halldix being a tinker wasn't bad enough, she had seen the state in which they kept their sorcerers in the Lordship of Fingers. She had read the reports but nothing prepared her for the reality: clusters of humans subsisting on barely enough food in shacks, with scant clothing to keep out the chill. Cassie wasn't sure if such conditions were deliberate callousness or merely a lack of knowledge about what humans required to live and thrive. Some were just children; with no one to train them how to navigate the otherworld, it was little wonder that the octopoids hadn't made much of an impact on the spirit activity at Oswego.

Each night after dinner, she would return to her private tent to take account of the day's labors. She had collected quite a range of spirits in their short time here, which only piqued her interest in finding Moonstone. Each night, the soldiers combed the area where it was deposited with the UV light, and each morning, they reported nothing found. Her forays and inquiries in the otherworld drew a blank. In her impatience, she called in an old friend three days into the search, hoping he could find what the Order of the Guard with an UV light could not.

Ryland was a rare breed in the church: a tinker-runner. The Church of Parkour employed tinkers to keep their technology functioning, but normally safeguarded them behind tall, thick walls where they could do their work in peace, and more importantly, safety. While some tinkers are born that way, others acquired their skills later on in their lives through nanite infestations which often resulted in a coma. However, not all who were exposed become tinkers; many just died, either immediately from shock or simply never waking from their coma. Ryland was one of the lucky ones. Not only did he survive after touching a pool of gray goo during a ruin run, the church still allowed him to run, using his new sight and abilities to collect tech from the rubble of the ancients. If anyone could find Moonstone using tech, Ryland could—he moved like a tracer but thought like a tinker.

Cassie approached her tent after securing her latest prize and found Ryland waiting patiently, sheltered from the worst of the wind. She bade him enter and held the flap open for him. "Tell me you have good news." Cassie vigorously rubbed her hands together to bring back warmth to her fingertips.

Ryland shed his heavy cloak and posited a rhetorical question, "Would you rather have good news or the truth?"

Cassie's face fell. "You didn't find it."

"Nope, I didn't find it," he confirmed, "but it wasn't from a lack of trying." He shed more layers as Cassie offered him a drink. "I can only speak for myself, but I'm damn good at what I do and if I can't find it with tech and you can't find it with sorcery, isn't it more likely that it's just not here?" He sipped the warm drink greedily. *Tea?* He knew it was serious if Cassie was abstaining from alcohol.

"I *know* it was here. Even if I were tempted to chalk up the sheer number of spirits to untamed ruins, some of them are just bizarre—like nothing I've seen before. I just don't know what happened to it and where it is now." Cassie absentmindedly stroked her pendant over her clothes. "There is one possibility, but I'll need your help."

"Anything for an old friend." Ryland leaned back in his chair, letting his feet get warm by the fire.

"And your quick acceptance has nothing to do with otherwise being assigned to Chicago in winter?" Cassie teased him.

"Why can't it be both?!" Ryland replied. "Don't spoil the moment. I can always tell when you have a corker of an idea." Cassie scribbled a quick note on some parchment and handed it to Ryland with instructions. The tinker-runner shook his head, weighing which was worse: Cassie's plan or wintering in Chicago. He donned his protective outer gear and exited the tent.

In the quiet moments before her standard evening engagement, Cassie fished out the small lacquered mahogany box inlaid with pearl runes and ran her fingers over the smooth lines of the recently made containment chamber. As soon as she found Moonstone, they could be on their way home where she could sleep in her own bed, avoid state dinners with tentacled nobles, and have all the time in the world to uncover the lunar meteorite's secrets. *Where the hell are you, Moonstone?* She cursed as she stuffed the box back into one of the many pockets hidden in the folds of her robes and got to work.

Cassie knew it all came down to timing. It wouldn't be hard to sell that spirit activity was behind the illness; after all, it was technically true, but its onset and the arrival of help from the church had to look organic—the appearance of an ally rather than a conspirator.

The sorcerer gathered the crucial components in a small brazier and lit the fire. She placed a small dish of honey and milk on the table before starting her incantations. The spell was not difficult, but required a certain level of finesse which was hard to muster after the brutal encounter this afternoon. She focused her fatigued mind and located its quiet center. The otherworld wasn't just spirits of the once living, but also creatures native to that realm. It was those beings that Cassie hoped to lure with the promise of milk and sweets, putting out the spiritual equivalent of a help wanted sign.

Not long after she started, a sprite appeared, sniffing the honey in the dish. Cassie addressed the fey in the language across the veil and struck her bargain. The winged spirit hungrily lapped up the milk and honey as a sign of agreement.

At least tonight's dinner will be more bearable, Cassie thought to herself as she put her tools away and dressed for dinner. Cassie practiced her poker face in the mirror—she'd need it when she watched the rubbery arms of the octopoid consume the food touched by the sprite that only she could see—none of the octopoid's slave-sorcerers were allowed to be in the same accommodations with him, much less dine at his table. Naturally, she would have to eat a little, just to throw off suspicion, but the church must remain unassailable. All she had to do was wait for the cavalry and hope they would answer her summons. *What has begun cannot be undone.*

Chapter Seven

All the pathfinders breathed a collective sigh of relief when Applied Tenets of Faith was canceled for the day. Apparently, no one was up for strikes, takedowns, and pins today. Instead, all four instructors would be demonstrating rituals in the ruins. Spending the afternoon outdoors on a rare sunny-if-cold day seemed less daunting than working the mats.

Rituals were as close to magical thinking as the Church of Parkour allowed. Strictly speaking, the church did not have deities they appeased, beseeched, or worshipped. Devotees of the faith adhered to a philosophy with the end goal of escaping the confines of existence under the shattered moon. Theology aside, the church offered stability and a frame of reference in an otherwise chaotic, barbaric world. In its infinite practicality, the church found ways to incorporate sentients of all stripes in its doctrine and practice: sorcerers and tinkers, scholars and runners, plebs and royals. However, in ritual, the Church of Parkour was singularly unique.

When a collection of like-minded individuals gathered together and focused their stillness, they could affect things around them. The most conspicuous display was the church's holdings themselves—they were almost always placed among ruins, yet within their domain, the ruins did not change or regenerate. Granted, this feat required the highest level of ritual and constant upkeep, thus the importance of morning devotion, which effectively anchored the area in its time and place. There were also smaller rituals that a sept could employ on a run.

Chandi took her seat in the circle and assumed the posture: seated with legs crossed, hands on knees with palms up, thumb and third digit in opposition. Chandi had witnessed some of these during her clandestine run to Oswego two months ago, the sacred mantras inextricably linked with the excitement of running unchartered ruins. When she closed her eyes and thought hard on it, she could almost imagine she was there again, hurdling over and under debris in the moonlight amidst the sept of tracers, cheeks flush from exertion and the night breeze.

As she daydreamed, her thoughts circled back to her nightmare. While it hadn't returned, she couldn't let it go. It may have started out as a memory of her early training—the church certainly ascertained the limits of her abilities and how she could cope with the biofeedback from exposure—but it quickly turned into something else. It felt like a cry for help or maybe a warning—full of looming danger, panic, and powerlessness. Everyone at the king's estate attributed it to the recent attack on the envoy, but Chandi wasn't so certain. It felt personal. For the first time in months, Chandi wondered where Moonstone was and, in spite of all the disruption it'd caused in the Monastery of Unseen Waters, she couldn't help hoping it was all right.

Chandi flinched as a rock landed squarely on her back. "The ritual works better *when everyone is focusing* their stillness," Netu rebuked from the sidelines. Chandi centered her mind, cultivating the bead of stillness within and expanding it as she repeated the mantra, not in voice but in mind. She couldn't be certain it worked, but she didn't feel the ping of another projectile. For now, that was enough.

*****

Jackson was putting the finishing touches on his spell when he heard a knock on his door. The sorcerer eyed it suspiciously; late-night visitors were rarely good news when you're the on-site otherworld specialist. He steeled himself for what waited for him on the other side of the door.

He was greeted by a scruffy figure wrapped in layers of clothing still chilled from the blustery night. A familiar voice and smirk emerged from under the hood, "Are you going to let me in or do I have to drink this whiskey all by myself?"

"Ry?" Jackson asked quizzically. The sorcerer immediately reached out and embraced him, flinching only as an afterthought. Ryland was Jackson's friend long before he became infested with nanites, and he was the only exception to Jackson's strict avoidance of tinkers and technology. Even still, the idea of all those nanites crawling on him gave him the creeps. "Come in and get warm." Jackson stepped aside and shuffled things around the room for his unexpected visitor.

Ryland shed his outer layers in the relative warmth of the room but kept his gloves on out of respect for his sorcerous friend. Jackson found two cleanish tumblers and set them up for the aforementioned spirits. As Ryland drew back his hood, Jackson scowled. "What is that thing on your face?"

"You like it?" Ryland stroked the hair under his lower lip. "I'm trying something new."

"It looks like something died on your chin."

"Then it's a good thing I can shave it off whenever I like; too bad there's nothing that can be done about your ugly mug," he quipped.

Jackson let Ryland settle into his seat with a cup before he indulged his curiosity. "So, what brings you to my neck of the woods? Not that I'm not glad to see you, but they don't usually send a tracer to inspect and repair the tech, even they are also a tinker."

"I was in the neighborhood helping out a mutual friend," he answered neutrally. Something tingled in Jackson's brain; Ryland always had a good poker face.

"And this mutual friend would be?"

Ryland took a long drink before he spoke; he knew he was diving into deep and troubled waters. "Cassie's in trouble, and she needs your help."

Jackson gave him a dubious look. "Cassie would rather walk barefoot over hot coals before asking me for help."

"Which should tell you how much of a pickle she's in."

"I'm going to need another drink," Jackson grumbled as he poured. "So what has Cassie gotten herself into this time?"

"She's lost something. From what I gather, it's pretty important."

"And she thinks I'll be able to help her find it? When we were together, she was the one who knew where everything was," Jackson took a stab at humor; it beat anger or depression, which were his only other options and he had done his time in both of those.

Ryland, who had been there for the entire saga, merely laughed. "She thought you might be hesitant, so I'm to relay a message before you give your final answer." He fished something out of one of his many pockets—tinkers, the only sentients under the shattered moon with as many pockets as sorcerers. Jackson unfurled the scrap of paper: *Moonstone. Bring pathfinder. Quick.*

"Well, shit," Jackson muttered under his breath and finished his drink.

*****

Chandi couldn't breathe, she couldn't speak, she couldn't think. She just kept moving, every muscle in her body taut with pent-up energy. The well of tension grew until she could no longer contain it and it erupted, sending ripples of kinetic release through her whole body. Beads of sweat glistened on her hazelnut skin as she dropped to her side. She retrieved the blanket that had slid down to her hips; she wanted to savor the warmth they had created. "Welcome home," she murmured.

Mika nuzzled against her. "Certainly beats extra raisins in my porridge," he teased.

Chandi pulled away and punched his arm. "Keep talking like that and porridge is the only warm thing you'll get your hands on." Mika placed a delicate kiss on her shoulder as way of an apology, and Chandi let him slide his arm around her waist and pull her closer.

Nestled in the crook of his arm, she examined his bare chest, smooth to the touch except for three aspiring chest hairs. In a mischievous moment, she had given them names. Mika threatened to pluck them when she told him about Larry, Moe, and Curly, but she stood by them—anything that stubbornly strove to exist in such a barren landscape deserved to be acknowledged. Her fingertips lightly grazed the seam of coarse skin—a knitted scar from a long-ago injury. Mika told her it didn't hurt anymore, but he winced the first time she stroked it. Now, he simply caressed her back with his hand.

His breathing evened out and she could feel its cadence in her hair. She angled her head up. "Do you think you'll be here for Longest Night?"

Mika shook his head noncommittally. "I don't have another assignment before the new year, but you know how it is—if I'm called, I go where I'm needed."

"Bleah," she blurted disdainfully and subconsciously pushed away for more space.

"Something wrong?"

"What does that even mean? Who's deciding what's needed where?" Chandi's irritation caused her voice to raise more than she had intended.

"Is this about training? Are you having problems with your preceptor?" he probed cautiously while continuing to rub her back with long fluid strokes.

"No, Dora's pretty cool," Chandi replied, tight-lipped about her changing relationship with the church. Chandi hadn't told any of her friends about it. She wasn't against taking counsel, but she knew everyone would have an opinion and she wanted a better handle on her own thoughts before she declared open season on advice.

"The time of declaration is coming up, is that it?" Mika nudged. "You wouldn't be the first to struggle with whether to continue training toward tracer or just running as a pathfinder."

"Really?"

"Sure!" Mika breathed a sigh of relief; he took Chandi's

genuine surprise as an indication that he'd finally guessed right and Chandi didn't bother to correct him. "There's a reason the church pushes so hard toward becoming a tracer—everyone goes a little crazy at the prospect of freedom."

"Why did you decide to become a tracer?"

Mika shrugged. "When I really thought about it, being a pathfinder wasn't for me. I would get bored running the same ruins with the same sentients. And if you think getting told when and where to go as a tracer stinks, just imagine what it would be like being part of the local politics of a sept. If you got unlucky and were stuck in a bad situation, you'd just have to make the best of it. As a tracer, you're only there for a short time and then you're gone. Why do you think Dora returned for training?"

Chandi propped herself up on one arm. "*She's* the pathfinder that returned for tracer training?!"

"Yeah. She's a few years older than me, but I remember her. I imagine they don't advertise that fact—they don't want everyone to leave with the delusion that they'll just come back when they're ready." Chandi settled back down. "The truth is, once you leave, it becomes a million times harder to return. Right now, you are used to being a student but once you leave, the more ridiculous aspects of training stand out and chafe."

Chandi let all this sink in. She'd always assumed she would continue with tracer training—that was what she was always told was the next step on the right path. Then she'd experienced the exhilaration of night running to Oswego amidst a sept of tracers—would it always be like that or would it grow routine as well? And now that she had options, the future seemed less clear-cut.

"Have you ever thought about leaving the church?" Chandi asked as casually as she could.

"Are you serious?" Mika turned his head to look at her but the shadows from the dim light hid most of her face. "The world under the shattered moon is brutal. Better to align yourself with a group. The Church of Parkour may not be perfect, but at least it takes care of its own."

Chandi shivered as she recalled the failed ambush, the blood-splattered abbess, and the indifferent way she'd cleaned herself of that blood. She quickly changed the subject. "What's it like out there? In the ruins?"

"It's not like it is in Watertown. Even when things get hairy, you know you have Unseen Waters close by. You have the instructors and tracers and other trainees. When you are out there as a tracer, you are on your own, left to your own devices. The sept you are running with might have your back, but you can't always count on that. But when you are maneuvering through the rubble, you'll never feel more alive and free." Somewhere between the words, Mika had stopped stroking her back. He looked down to find Chandi watching him intently. Her emerald eyes were dark in the low light.

"Anyone ever tell you your nose twitches when you talk

about running?" She had just a hint of a curve in the corners of her mouth.

"That's funny...I could have sworn I felt something else twitch." Chandi let out a high-pitched squeal as Mika pulled her under him. The blanket roiled from the commotion underneath when a crisp knock fell on Mika's door. They immediately stilled and waited. Mika felt the rise and fall of Chandi's chest against his as she breathed, her soft fragrant skin brushing his before retreating again and again.

"Ignore it. Maybe they'll go away?" Mika whispered as his lips made contact with hers and his hand moved down to her hips. At that moment, Chandi could not find fault in his logic.

And then another set of raps followed, this time less timid and more insistent. Mika grunted as he tore himself from bed. "I'll be right back." Chandi giggled under the covers as she heard him stumble into his clothes.

Mika answered the door brusquely only to be greeted by the numerous eyes of the prioress. "Pardon the intrusion, Brother Mika, but would Pathfinder Choudary happen to be inside? The abbess seeks audience with her and she's not in her room..."

*****

The snow had ceased for the moment, but their trek did not. The Laughter at the End of Time stood a thousand strong, fed on the cellars and slaughtered of Kemptville, and warmed by the burning embers of what remained. Their victory boosted morale and, even Terem had to admit that this felt good and right. In the course of battle, leadership shifted once again in the constant flux of power that reigned among in the ruin dwellers.

Like locusts, they set their sights on their next meal across the river, but only the old knew the danger that lay ahead. The Saint Lawrence River froze every year, but it was early days…had the hard ice set? That was the gamble that Hrok took, and it was only proper that the strong should lead the way. He took his first steps on the ice with confidence, as if it would not dare buckle beneath his feet. The crackles and pings reverberated with each step and it was only when he put some distance between himself and the shore that he could hear the true song of the ice. The metallic hum buzzed in his ears and its eerie harmonics were melodic in their own way. It was almost beautiful in this stark setting and stirred something deep in Hrok's memory, like a mother's song. It was the last thing Hrok heard before he crashed through the thin ice, carried beneath a crystalline sheet by the current into a watery tomb.

Chapter Eight

Chandi whipped around the room in search of things to stuff in her backpack while Lucy watched from Chandi's bed. "First the prioress comes looking for you in the middle of the night and now you're packing…what's going on?"

"I can't tell you," Chandi answered as she picked through their shared toiletries, taking only what she needed.

"Where are you going?" Lucy probed.

"I can't say," Chandi replied absentmindedly as opened and closed another drawer.

"When will you be back?" Lucy tried again.

Chandi sighed. "I don't know." She hated keeping things from Lucy. She couldn't tell her she chose to go—that she had a choice now—or that Moonstone was that dangerous and close to her. When did things get so complicated that you couldn't tell your best friend everything?

"Can you at least tell me if Mika is still as hot as ever?" Lucy asked pointedly.

The pathfinder paused. "Yes. I can definitely tell you he is. I can also verify that arachnids are not his thing." Chandi held her arm up and let it drop precipitously. Lucy failed to stifle a guffaw and Chandi had a moment of clarity—who could she trust under the shattered moon more than Lucy? "I promise I'll tell you as much as I can when I get back. Good enough?"

"Do I have a choice?" Lucy answered sullenly.

"I'll decorate ornaments with you every night until the entire monastery sparkles on Longest Night and we'll catch up. Promise," Chandi conceded.

Lucy accepted her offer. "What are you looking for?"

"My heavy sweater." Chandi swore, exasperated. Lucy stood up off of Chandi's bed and handed her the thick woolen garment from beneath her. "That was a dirty trick."

"I knew you wouldn't leave without it. At least I warmed it up for you." Lucy embraced her in a hug. "Be careful…you won't have a seven-foot tigress with you this time." Suddenly, Chandi realized the tribute attack had violated more than just her own sense of safety.

She hugged Lucy a little harder. "Save plenty of glitter and glue for when I come home."

As Chandi finished packing, Jackson was arranging his own gear. From Ryland's account, it sounded like Cassie had a good handle on the spirits, but her message was less than illuminating. Knowing Cassie, she did that on purpose; her personal motto was "always leave them wanting more." The sorcerer grabbed the intricately carved horn from a shelf and wrapped it in soft linen—better to be safe than sorry.

Ryland took the opportunity to replenish his supplies with the cook and quartermaster rather than grab a few winks of sleep. There would be time for that on the way to Oswego. The tinker relished the thought of a carriage ride and thanked the fates that Jackson was no runner.

Khiri paced as the captain of the Order of the Guard once more went over the route and guard detail for the impromptu envoy west. There was debate on how much force was necessary; even though the Lordship of Fingers was technically at war with the Kingdom of a Thousand Islands, there hadn't been fighting between them for years. On the other hand, the church was sending three valuable church members into the territory of a relatively new and tenuous diplomatic contact.

The knot in the abbess's stomach refused to unwind, and it had little to do with Aren's impeccable planning. She had her reservations about sending Chandi out so soon after the attack on the tribute carriage, but the pathfinder was no longer a child and she left the decision to her. While Khiri could not accompany her longtime ward, she took some comfort that Jackson and Ryland would be there. They may be yahoos, but they were competent yahoos that knew better than to disappoint the abbess. The gloom of the thick cloud cover did little to lift Khiri's mood as the carriage left the monastery gates with two squads in the dim haze of the early morning.

*****

Cassie cursed her scheming before heaving another course of bitter bile. The acidic burn tickled the back of her throat, making her cough uncontrollably. Her shoulders and chest ached from the jarring and she could feel a warm flush come over her face as it broke a sweat. Her hair was matted to her face and neck.

Looking back, Cassie conceded that her plan could have been better thought out. Perhaps it would have been better to use something other than a fey creature; even the best of them have a penchant for mischief, and their otherworldly constitution gives them a slightly skewed concept of "a little sick." Perhaps she should not have eaten as much of the tainted food in her quest of remaining above suspicion. More concerning was Halldix's condition. From all accounts, he was worse off than Cassie and the octopoids refused any treatment measures offered by the church. They insisted on using "their ways," which included things like bleeding the bad blood with leeches. If Halldix died on her, this entire diplomatic mission would be an unmitigated disaster—no Moonstone, no relationship with the Lordship of Fingers. But hindsight was a luxury no one had in the moment.

Look on the bright side, Cassie thought to herself. *If you die, you can't take the heat for this one.* She cackled at her gallows humor. Cassie failed to hear the sound of an approaching carriage over her coughing and lamenting, but she stirred at the cool breeze as the flap of her tent opened, letting in some fresh air and diluting the sour smell of sick. She felt someone place a hand to her forehead and opened her eyes. "I know you." Her voice cracked on the upward lilt. She raised her hand only to lose steam halfway up.

Jackson caught her arm and placed it around his neck. "It's okay, Cassie. I've got you. It's time to go back to bed. I need you to help me. Hold on as tight as you can, okay?" Jackson picked her up off the floor; her body sagged in his arms. Jackson looked to Ryland and Chandi. "You got any ideas?"

Chandi looked around the room; her innate abilities to purify disease would take time, but she had spent enough hours in Unseen Water's infirmary to pick up a thing or two. The soldiers did their best to care for Cassie, but they were clearly more familiar with the end of the spear than a sick bed. "Put her here." She motioned toward the cot. Chandi threw out the stagnant water and vomit, then poured pure water from her canteen into a clean basin and hunted down a fresh rag to wipe down Cassie's feverish face. "We need to get some fluid in her." She handed her canteen to Ryland. "There should be more water in there, but be sure to screw the cap on tight afterward. Put on a kettle and make some weak tea. Add some salt and sugar to it, maybe a little honey if there is any." Ryland set to work as Chandi closed her eyes and sang a song in her mind, fighting back her own waves of nausea.

Cassie drifted in and out of consciousness, and each time she woke, Chandi spooned morsels of warm tea into her parched mouth. Eventually, she was able to take small sips when the cup was brought to her lips. As Chandi's nausea improved, so did Cassie's condition until the fever broke; only then did Cassie's body find restful slumber.

Jackson and Ryland stood a tense watch over Chandi and her patient—this situation was out of their wheelhouse and it drove them to distraction in their own way. Ryland's curiosity got the better of him as he poked around Cassie's tent before turning his attention to the seemingly endless supply of fresh water coming out of Chandi's canteen. After some creative prodding, he discovered the freshwater pearl at the bottom. The tinker whistled in appreciation. *Kid's got friends in high places to have one of these before she's even done with pathfinder training.*

Once Cassie was stable, Jackson turned to her journal and tried to make sense of what had happened in the few days since Ryland left her. Most was bookkeeping regarding supplies and captured spirits, but he found one notation toward the later entries. *Oh Cassie, what did you get yourself into?*

Jackson closed the tome and took stock of the room: Chandi had fallen asleep in the chair beside the cot while Ryland was having a smoke. He ceremoniously suited up, checking each pocket, shining his belt buckle, and securing his sheathed dagger. Ryland caught a glimpse of Jackson's face and knew all too well what it meant. Ryland continued to smoke but made sure his pistol was nearby. Jackson turned and gave him a nod, and Ryland returned the gesture. They didn't need words to say what was happening next. Jackson was going to take care of a problem; Ryland was going to keep them safe until he returned.

It was the dead of night when Jackson strode out of Cassie's tent. The morning's overcast had passed and pinpoints of starlight cascaded across the sky, outshone only by the sliver of the shattered moon. Despite his anger, he managed to find a speck of silence in the cacophony of the otherworld. He followed the spiritual trail and as he neared the octopoids, he raised his light source and directed the beam onto his Church of Parkour tabard. His sorcerous murmuring and purposeful stride was enough to gain passage through their encampment—*that vertebrate was either crazy or inspired!* Either way, he was a man with a plan; best not to get in his way.

Jackson stopped outside of Halldix's quarters to a fan of spears. He raised the light to his face, grim and serious. "If you want any hope that he will live, you'll let me help." The hardened octopoid militia had discipline and held their ground. "Fine, we'll do this the hard way."

Jackson backed away from the tent, took a handful of sawdust from one pocket, and started his incantation. With each crescendo, he thrust another heap of sawdust before him, coaxing the sprite out from its hiding place. It was only a matter of time and will. He had a name—that was all he needed. The screeching that came from within Halldix's quarters startled the octopoids guarding their ailing lord. None were inside except the healers, who suddenly fled from the doorway.

A small winged creature soon followed, lassoed tight by blue spectral bands that dragged him out of Halldix's quarters. "Eivult, approach and be judged for your deeds," Jackson commanded the resistant fey, who writhed and wailed the whole way. The light from the bands burned brighter the harder the sprite fought, eliciting howls of pain at its searing touch.

"I have broken no oath!" it cried in the tongue of the otherworld.

Jackson drew his dagger. "I have no oath with you." The sorcerer plunged his blade into its skull, nearly cutting the creature in half. The piercing death bawl reached registers beyond Jackson's hearing as the speck of light that once was Eivult plunged into his belt buckle. A stunned dark quiet fell over the octopoids as the sorcerer addressed them communally in a loud voice. "A healer from the Church of Parkour has come to heal our stricken. I know not if her power will work on your sick, but she may be willing to try if she is welcomed to your settlement." With that, Jackson turned around and headed back into the ruins of Oswego.

Chapter Nine

Chandi stared blankly at the three-inch hole in the wall. It was as close to Halldix as the octopoids would allow her. Only invertebrates could breech his quarters through such a small entrance. Her nausea was stronger here and lasted longer; she only hoped that small hole was enough for her to purify the sickness from him. This was her second vigil in as many days; if she had known she was going to be performing infirmary duty, she would have brought a book.

With Ryland and the squad of the Order of the Guard just outside, the quiet solitude gave her time to think. She ruminated over all the trips she'd made to Dexter's estate, the various savories and sweets Chef Pasleur had fed her over the years, and all the books she had yet to read. She replayed tea with Emma in her head.

Up until now, Chandi had never thought about if she wanted to have a family. Marriage and babies were not part of her daily existence in the monastery; wanting that didn't even seem like an option. It's not that she wanted to get pregnant right this second, but feeling the little punches and kicks from

Emma's womb struck her deeply. Her mother once told her life must fight its way into being, and that sucker was ready to live. Could she see herself married or with children? Maybe. Someday. But not as long as she was running for the church.

She touched her lotus pendent and tried to remember her village, what her parents looked like, and how big their cottage seemed when she was little. She considered what she was going to tell Lucy and how to even start. She recalled Mika's warmth; his scent still on her skin, albeit faintly.

Throughout the day, rubbery-skinned octopoids entered and left through the aperture, paying little-to-no mind to the pathfinder, contorting their bodies into impossibly narrow dimensions with ease. When no one was watching, Chandi would stare through the gap and catch small glimpses of her patient on the other side of the wall. A mass of mottled flesh reclined on a raised platform. Pillows propped up its bulbous hump while each of its eight limbs sprawled in all directions. Occasionally, one of them would move. The bowl of leeches sat by the bed with streaks of blue from their meals. Chandi knew little about octopoid physiology and hoped that was normal, for Halldix's sake.

She surfed the waves of nausea and when they got particularly bad, she sang aloud. She had reached the part in her song where an avatar of Ganesha removed the large stone that blocked a cave mouth so the girl could take shelter during a storm, when her stomach calmed down and she ceased her ballad.

"Don't stop. It's beautiful," a weak voice came from the other side of the hole.

Chandi leapt up from her seat. "You're up! I should get your healers."

"Please don't!" Halldix entreated. "They'll just put more leeches on me." Chandi heard a distinct sigh. "Just stay a little longer and keep singing. I find it soothing."

Chandi took all this as a generally positive sign and restarted where she'd left off. She made a mental note for future reference: octopoids have blue blood.

*****

Cassie held the bowl of warm broth to her lips and drank hungrily; it was the first time in days her empty stomach accepted anything. "Slow down. Chandi said to start feeding you *slowly*. The last thing we want is more vomiting," Jackson cautioned. He handed her some crackers to dip in the thin soup and nibble. They tasted like cardboard, but Chandi said "bland" and there was nothing that tasted less interesting than hardtack.

"It's a good thing you already have a job, because you make a pretty miserable nurse," Cassie commented between bites.

Jackson smirked. "You must be feeling better if you have the energy to throw a few punches." He wiped his hands and took a seat beside her cot. He pulled out his knife and a piece of wood he started carving to pass the time.

"Where is Chandi?" Cassie inquired.

"Tending to Lord Kepoi."

Cassie sat up and her eyes widened. "They gave her an audience?!"

Jackson shrugged. "After the light show I gave them, I suggested that if they wanted him to live, they should be nice to our 'healer.'"

Her brow furrowed. "You didn't send her alone, did you?"

"Do I look stupid? Don't answer that," Jackson quickly added. "I sent her with Ry and a squad of well-armed guards to encourage cooperation." Cassie reclined on her stack of pillows with a relieved look. "I told him to get her the hell out of there if the octopus isn't better by the end of the day. Last thing she needs is to become the scapegoat for his death. Assuming killing him wasn't part of the plan…"

Cassie glanced at Jackson's face for signs of disapproval or recrimination but found none. They both knew his words were enough. She squared her shoulders stubbornly. "I don't need to explain myself to you," she stated defensively.

"No," Jackson replied gently, "but when you ask for my help and drag me out to the middle of nowhere, it's the polite thing to do."

Cassie could have handled his anger, judgment, or yelling, but his quiet patience broke her. Her frame slumped. "I've made a mess of everything, haven't I?"

"You may have overdone it," he euphemistically rephrased her words before switching to the sorcerous tongue. "Just start at the beginning."

Cassie started talking while Jackson whittled, giving his hands and eyes something to focus on so as not to disrupt her retelling. "I was running out of time and I had to find a way to stall," she concluded. "She's the only sentient Moonstone had any sort of connection with. This may be the only shot I get; I couldn't leave without trying everything." Jackson had finished his figurine, a squirrel with an acorn between its hands. He was still processing Cassie's dilemma when the flap opened to Ryland and Chandi's return.

"You're up," Chandi stated the obvious as she shed layers in the warm tent. She looked around the room. "And eating. That's good. How do you feel?"

"Better, thanks to you." Chandi gave an awkward bow; she was trying to get better at accepting thanks and praise. It was a work in progress.

"Well, Lord Kepoi is on the mend. When we left their settlement, he was awake and strong enough to refuse more leech treatment." Chandi poured herself a cup of something warm. "Did you know they have blue blood?"

"It's the copper," Ryland answered. "We have iron in our blood and they have copper." The three of them gawked at him. "What...I can't know things? These aren't the first sentients of octopus lineage I've come across."

Cassie sat back up with fire in her voice. "And you didn't think to tell me this earlier?!"

Ryland wobbled his head ambiguously. "You didn't ask. You had your stacks of briefings and reports, so I figured you knew all you needed to know. Plus, you brought me here to find something, not liaison with the squishy many-armed."

"I don't know how you've put up with him so long!" Cassie swore in the language of the otherworld. Jackson chuckled.

"They're speaking in their special language—they can only be up to no good!" Ryland joked.

"Maybe he can help figure out what happened to Moonstone," Jackson answered Cassie in kind.

Chandi froze amidst the friendly bilingual banter. "Did you say 'Moonstone'?"

Cassie and Jackson stared at her. "Did you hear 'Moonstone'?" he replied carefully. It was the first time he had ever had a non-human understand the otherworld speech.

Ryland felt the tension ramp up acutely. "It sounded like a bunch of gibberish to me," he said off-handedly.

"Me too, except for that last bit. I heard 'Moonstone,'" Chandi confessed.

"We need to have a talk—all cards on the table. Agreed?" Jackson's gaze went first to Cassie, who reluctantly nodded. Then to Chandi, who concurred. When he looked to Ryland, the tinker put his hands up, indicating he had nothing to hide.

Jackson went to the entrance, motioned for more guards, and secured the flap.

Their caucus lasted well into the evening. Cassie shared the elder council's plans for Moonstone as a diplomatic tool to open relations with the Lordship of Fingers, and all that followed. Each had their chance to admire the beauty of the containment box, to rub their fingers over its intricate ruins. Chandi explained her inextricable link to Moonstone and her suspicions that it was in trouble and possibly underwater. Jackson made note of the spirits Cassie had already contained in Oswego—if Moonstone was still out there, it needed to be contained. Ryland shed some light on the octopoids: they communicate through changing colors in their skin at a much wider spectrum than typical sentient vision. They could see and produce colors in the UV spectrum.

Cassie swore. "That would have been nice to know before we painted Moonstone." Jackson and Chandi glared at her. "Okay, before *I* had Moonstone painted."

"It's not common knowledge, but it's not a closely guarded secret. If you had asked the right sentients—" Ryland tried his best to sound conciliatory.

"That's not the council's way. Founders forbid they admit they don't know everything," Cassie chewed off bitterly.

"What's done is done." Jackson steered the conversation to more solution-focused territory. "The question now is what are we going to do about it?"

"Look for it in Lake Ontario?" Chandi suggested. "We're standing on its shores and it's possible that Moonstone tumbled its way into the nearest body of water."

"That's not a bad idea," Jackson endorsed her idea, albeit with more surprise than was complimentary. "But that water is freezing—there is no way anyone could go diving until summer."

Ryland spoke up, "With the right gear, we could probably push that up to spring. I'm sure the elder council has enough pull to get its hands on some diving dry suits."

Cassie's face had that look that Jackson and Ryland knew all too well. She was planning something. "I have an idea."

Chapter Ten

Chandi sat by the fire, casting her eyes to the starlit sky. The ruins looked much the same as they had when she ran them a few months ago, although the circumstances were quite different then. Moonstone had been in her care, and her heart was lightened by the visit. This second time around, the thrill of covert, uncharted running was replaced by worry and dread.

Ryland stoked the fire and offered Chandi a cup. "It's going to be a long night, and this should take out the chill." The pathfinder took a sip and her face winced as the whisky burned down her throat.

"You think this is really going to work?" she asked, looking at the bucket of water sitting well outside the heat of the fire.

Ryland considered her question. "Why not? I've heard of crazier schemes."

"You seem rather nonchalant about this whole thing. I can only imagine how unbelievable it seems at first glance." A pleasant warmth spread to her cheeks, and Chandi decided to take another sip.

"Kid, when you've lived through what I have, not much

phases you."

"It's Chandi."

"What?"

"My name. It's Chandi. And I'm not a kid anymore."

"My mistake." Ryland took a swing from his cup to mask his smile.

"You're a tinker, right?"

"Yup."

"But you weren't born that way."

"What makes you say that?"

"Jackson and Cassandra. They don't take to tinkers, but they're all right with you, which means you guys have history. Which means there must have been a time when you didn't tinker." Ryland took note of her keen perception.

"Well, you're right. Sorcerers and tinkers are like water and oil, but some bonds are for keeps. We go back a long time—almost feels like another lifetime—but here we are plotting again, thick as thieves."

"But you also run?" Chandi circumambulated the edges of her curiosity.

"And how did you know that?"

"You move like a runner."

Ryland chuckled. "You're a regular Sherlock Holmes, aren't you?"

"If I am, I'm sorely missing my Watson," Chandi quipped back. Ryland nodded in appreciation—he could attribute her literary education to Brother Bartholomew, but the quick wit was all her own.

"To answer your question, yes, I am a tracer of the true path." Ryland sensed there was more to this but waited patiently. The silence between them grew and it felt like the whole sky was expanding into the night.

"How did you get the church to let you keep running?" Chandi blurted out bluntly. "I mean, usually they keep all that separate. How did you get to do both?"

"I didn't give them a choice. I'm both, and if the church wanted me, they had to accept both. I didn't let them choose which parts of me to selectively cut." Ryland looked over the fire to see if Chandi understood his words, but her furrowed brow suggested otherwise. "Chandi, it's like this. You've really only got one choice in life: are you in or are you out. There's no halfway. It's like jumping in the river: if you're in, you are going where the current takes you until you get out or go under. The trick is never to gamble what you aren't willing to lose. If you say you're out, you have to be okay with leaving. If it's a bluff and they call you on it, they've got you in the worse possible way."

Chandi thought on his mixed metaphor. "So they didn't call your bluff?" she guessed optimistically.

"Oh, they did. Told me I was to cease running and start tinker training, only I never showed up for that assignment." Ryland took another gulp. "I packed my things and headed to a small town I knew not far from some ruins I had run a couple of times. I knew they had a tinker there, and I made them a deal that worked for everyone. I could get in and out of the ruins better than any of them. I'd bring back valuable tech, and in exchange, I'd learn how to use my new friends from a seasoned tinker."

"Friends?"

"That's what I call my nanites. It sounds better than 'invaders' or 'parasites.'" Ryland winked in jest. "It took the church the better part of a year to reconsider their stance. It wouldn't surprise me if Cassie planted a few seeds in fertile soil—something along the lines of 'think of the value his tinker vision would bring to the type of salvage he brings back from runs.' She has a way of putting things so that her view always seems to be the reasonable one."

"So you went back?"

"Not at first, but eventually." There was a finality in his answer that signaled to Chandi that line of inquiry was over.

"Do they hurt—the nanites?" Chandi deftly changed topics, sensing his resistance.

"No, although sometimes they itch." Chandi couldn't tell if Ryland was serious or teasing her. "Wanna see something cool?" Chandi put down her empty cup and nodded. Ryland took off his right glove and showed her his empty hand in the fire light; with a flick of his wrist, a teeming mass of tiny black specks appeared and formed a solid wrench. He extended his arm. "Go on, you can hold it. It won't hurt."

Chandi hesitated. "And I won't get infested?"

Ryland chortled out loud, a warm and full honest laugh. "No, that's not how it works, although I would never do this with Jackson or Cassie. Water and oil, remember?"

Chandi picked up the tool from his hand, surprised by its weightiness. "It feels like a real wrench." She handed it back to him. He absorbed the tool back into his hand.

"It is a real wrench, just one that I'll never lose." He smiled at his private joke as his put his glove back on. Ryland stood up and checked on the bucket of water—just a few small crystals of ice, but far from chunky. His did some rough calculations in his head—it should be ready in a few hours, another two hours to freeze solid…that gave them two to three hours to run in, bury it in the snow, and run out before sunrise.

A deep yawn escaped Chandi's mouth as the fire crackled. "Why don't you get a couple of hours of shut eye and I'll get you when it's ready," Ryland offered.

"No, I'm okay," the pathfinder protested a little too adamantly.

Ryland wrapped a blanket around him. "Suit yourself, but I'm taking a nap. It's going to take them some time before they are ready for us, and running tired makes you sloppy. It's a sure-fire way to make mistakes."

"You promise to wake me when it's time?" Chandi demanded sharply.

"Cross my heart."

*****

Jackson dipped the ball in the warm wax, rolled it in the pile of salt, and waited for this layer to harden. Cassie was flipping through her journal, looking for the next spirit to incorporate. "What about the one with two autonomous heads?"

"Didn't one of those heads spit fire?" Jackson dubiously asked. "We want a lot of smoke but no fire, remember?"

Cassie harrumphed at his dismissal. "If it's too weak, they won't take note."

"Once bitten, twice shy," he cited the old maxim. "They just survived a lunar otherworld infestation and the relative calm after church intervention. They will be extra vigilant after we leave and raise the alarm at the first hint of more spirit activity."

Cassie couldn't argue with his logic. "Well, I suppose I could take that one back for study; should pique some interest." She flipped back further in her journal—something flashy, all bark and no bite. "We'll use a lightning bug," she announced victoriously. "Harmless enough for you?"

Jackson held out the ball for her to signal his approval. Cassie placed one hand on her amulet and the other on the globe. She closed her eyes and found the quiet within. Jackson watched an orb of light move from the lapis lazuli to their invention as Cassie finished her conjuration.

Jackson spotted signs of her exhaustion despite Cassie's efforts to push it back until the work was done. "Why don't I take the last one? Mix it up, so they don't get suspicious at seeing too many of the same spirits as before." Cassie nodded, relieved to have Jackson there. When you were a sorcerer, you were never really alone. The voices of the otherworld were always with you, but it was nice to have someone else in the room that heard them as well, even if they sometimes weren't the same voices.

Jackson repeated the process and waited for the next layer to cool. "You're sure the elder council is going to be okay with this?"

Cassie shrugged with indifference. "They voted to haunt the area in the first place, so I don't think they can take the moral high ground on this one."

"Hypocrisy has never stopped them before."

Cassie smiled. "No, but the tantalizing prospect for more should be enough. It's all in how you sell it."

Jackson placed one hand on his belt buckle and found the spirit he sought—the step fear would raise the octopoids' anxiety without an actual attack. The real danger there was the erratic things sentients did to each other when they were afraid and panicked. He murmured his spell and transferred the spirit with ease.

It was the first time he had loaded such a mundane thing

with a spirit—sorcerers typically enchanted finely made items to enhance them in some way. Even ever-lit candles were really nice, for candles. Jackson took a calculated risk, using Cassie's most expensive sealing wax and his rare sea salt; so far, it held and it just had to stay together for a few more months. When exposed to the elements, the topmost layer should dissolve and release a new spirit, each getting progressively more deadly. Jackson hoped the octopoids would ask for help before the orb was spent, for their sake.

Jackson applied a thin layer of glaze to seal in the top layer, both in awe and consternation at the thing they had made. Whoever thought of making a time-release spirit bomb? Cassie, that's who. He turned to address her, only to find her sleeping soundly. Once the ball was dry, he placed it into his pocket. Their work was done; the rest was up to Ryland and Chandi.

*****

Ryland jiggled the string that suspended the orb into the bucket and it was taut. The ice was finally set. Chandi watched as he eased the frozen block from its mold, wrapped it in coarse cloth, and trussed it with rope. His hands worked from muscle memory as he rigged the lines into a backpack.

He hoisted it onto Chandi's shoulders and tightened the straps to hold it against her body. "You sure you want to carry it?" he asked, double-checking before they took off.

"It's not too heavy." The pathfinder tested the distribution of weight on her frame.

"Okay, but no fancy maneuvers with that thing on your back. If it shifts off center…"

"Yes, granddad," Chandi teased him.

"Ha, ha," he replied drily. "We stick together and if we have to separate, you return to camp immediately and I'll take the long route to buy you some time."

"Got it."

"Ladies first." Ryland extended his arm and watched Chandi take off deeper into the ruins. They weren't going far, just enough to deflect suspicion away from the church; it wouldn't look good if the spirit bomb went off in the middle of their former camp. In all honesty, the pathfinder probably didn't need him to come along. She was young, strong, and full of piss and vinegar, but it was always safer to run in a pair than alone, and the abbess would not be pleased if something happened to Chandi.

Ryland sprinted to catch up and matched her pace. She was slowed by the extra weight, but had good form and clean execution based on the few obstacles they had to clear. He signaled to Chandi and they banked north toward Lake Ontario. They were hoping for a site closer to the water's edge so divers could get in and out of the lake unnoticed, but not too close as the shoreline might expand with spring melt. Ryland spied a sturdy oak that fit the bill.

Chandi carefully shed the block of ice to the ground and stretched out her unburdened back. Her warm breath steamed in the cold. "I told you it was heavy," Ryland chided as he undid the rope and packed the base of the tree with snow for insulation and camouflage.

"It's fine." She brushed off her aches and his concern with aplomb. "Nothing the run back won't fix." Ryland took out his knife and carved their initials in the tree: RS + CC. To any incidental onlookers, it would simply look like the mark of two lovers, but to Cassie, it would signal where to dig up the spirit bomb should the octopoids call for help early on.

Ryland didn't really feel old until they ran back toward their camp. He watched Chandi vault over some rubble with glee. She was doing it because she could; he was at the age where he constantly ran the numbers to conserve energy. It wasn't that he couldn't do the work, but he spent more for the effort and was acutely aware that his pool was diminishing. Her pool wasn't even completely filled yet.

Breaking down camp took the better part of the morning, despite their early start. Chandi and Ryland were consuming the last of the coffee, staving off the chill from their late-night deposit into the heart of Oswego. Morale was high among the troops—they were going home with a stopover at Unseen Waters. What the monastery lacked in luxury, it made up for cozy comforts: warm meals, hot showers, and plenty of cider.

The Order of the Guard were securing cargo and checking

all the ties when an entourage approached the edge of the ruins. The numerous arms of four octopoid soldiers bore a simple palanquin while their unencumbered compatriots, brandishing weapons, flanked the vessel on all sides. Within moments, Cassie emerged in full Church of Parkour regalia to greet their visitors.

"Did you know they were coming?" Ryland muttered under his breath as they stepped into formation.

"Not a clue," Cassie answered, "but two can play at pageantry." Jackson and Ryland took positions behind Cassie with Chandi behind them. The Order of the Guard fell into rank and file, arms to their side but not far from ready.

The envoy halted before Cassie. The octopoids lowered the support poles, placing the palanquin closer to the ground. Two suckered limbs drew back the curtain while another made the pronouncement, "Presenting Lord Halldix Kepoi, son of Thenor, of the Lordship of Fingers."

Halldix glided out of the box. His burgundy color was dotted with white spots circled in black and yellow. An iridescent flourish started at his hump before rippling over this skin down all eight of his limbs. His militia knelt before his display. The diamond of Church of Parkour members followed Cassie's lead in a deep formal bow while the Order of the Guard stood at attention. Cassie kept the octopoids in her peripheral vision.

After an appropriate amount time, Cassie rose and spoke,

"You grace us with your presence, Lord Kepoi."

The octopoid noble stepped forward and shook two extended tentacles locked together. "I have heard of great deeds performed by the Church of Parkour on our behalf, and felt compelled to greet you once more before your departure."

More likely, he's making sure we are really leaving, Cassie thought to herself. "The Church of Parkour is glad to be of service to the Lordship of Fingers. We have done what we can under the circumstances to improve conditions, but this problem will need constant tending. We humbly extend our friendship and future aid should His Tentacled Majesty, in his infinite wisdom, deem it worthwhile." Ryland was the only one among them familiar enough with octopoid facial features to catch the hint of Halldix's sardonic smile.

"I will bear your well wishes myself, but first, I would like to address your healer." Jackson and Ryland exchanged sideways looks before stepping forward with Chandi. "Your presence was as refreshing as your song, and for your service, I present you with a pearl of making. I believe your people call it a 'freshwater pearl.'" There was only the slightest trace of condescension in his reference to the vertebrates.

Halldix produced a large gray pearl in the center of one of his suckers. "Unlike those that we produce for trade, this is an exquisite piece that you can turn on and off with thought." He twisted his tentacle and a fountain of water briefly flowed from the gem before ceasing. "Much more convenient with an off-switch, don't you think?" he commented with a familiarity that would be unthinkable if he were not a noble.

Halldix straightened himself and reinstated the dignity of his station. "Let it be known that you have done me a great service and when you present it, you will be known as a friend to the Lordship of Fingers." Halldix extended the tentacle and released the large gray pearl into Chandi's open palm. Its size and heft made an impression as it landed in her hand. She clutched the pearl and bowed deeply. Halldix released a bright streak of blue that scintillated down his body, and his militia echoed the display.

*****

"Well, you made quite an impression on Lord Kepoi," Cassie huffed as the carriage rolled toward Unseen Waters.

"All I did was sit next to small hole in the wall and not call his healers for more bleeding treatments when I figured out he was awake," Chandi qualified defensively. The urge to examine the gem was killing her, but she kept it safely tucked away in her pocket. The last thing she needed was to lose it in the carriage or bring down more of Cassie's ire.

"I mean, I cleared out the nastiest of spirits from his ruins and ate dinner with him every night, watching him eat with those tentacles and going on with his tinker prattle...no offense." She nodded to Ryland, who sat in the corner farthest from the sorcerers.

"None taken," he answered reflexively.

"I even got sick, but I didn't get a gift or a light show."

"To be fair, that illness was a product of your own machinations," Ryland reminded her.

"Yeah, but he didn't know that!" Cassie retorted.

"He's a tinker. I bet all his stuff is either tech or crawling with nanites," Jackson intervened. "Nothing fit for a sorcerer. Plus, diplomatic relations are open. That should please the elder council and buy you some latitude in the future." Cassie's annoyance lessened marginally.

"Let's see it," Ryland suggested as he pulled out a magnifying glass from one of his pockets and handed it to Chandi. "Don't you want to take a closer look, Sherlock?"

The pathfinder hesitated for a second but quickly dug out her prize. The gray sphere was perfectly smooth and round; the magnifying glass caught a beam of light that brought out its soft luster. It was at least twice as big as the one Brother Bartholomew had given her, with the added benefit of not gushing out water all over her hand. She handed it to Ryland to examine.

"It's a pretty piece of kit." Ryland rolled it around in his hand. "May even be a perfect sphere, which is rare to find in nature."

"It's a piece of tech, so it's not exactly natural," Jackson astutely commented. Cassie and Jackson kept their distance.

"Now that you have this newer, shinier version, mind if I examine your old pearl when we get back to Unseen Waters? I'd like to see if I can crack the method behind it."

"As long as you don't damage it," Chandi consented. "It was a gift from an old friend."

"Will you have the time?" Cassie interjected. She herself was only spending one night at the monastery before moving on.

"Before I left, the abbess roped me into agreeing to do maintenance and repairs before winter comes, so it looks like I'll be around for a while." Cassie gave him an amused glare from the other side of the carriage. "Don't worry, Chicago will still be there, and if it's not, you'll be really glad I wasn't there when it disappeared."

Chapter Eleven

Lucy whipped her hair into a knot before proceeding. She carefully traced the delicate pencil lines with a thin bead of glue, gentling squeezing the tube to capture each curve, scroll, and dot before spreading a layer of colorful glitter across the surface. The pattern reminded Chandi of the reddish brown henna designs on her mother's hands.

"Now what?" Chandi asked.

"Now we let it dry and shake off the excess for the next batch," Lucy explained while she dusted off as much glitter from her hands as she could before sweeping back an errant piece of hair from her eyes. "On to the next one!"

Chandi tried her hand at a simpler task: cutting out snowflakes from folded paper. It wasn't the intricate lace Lucy could produce, but it was adequately festive and gave Chandi a sense of awe each time she unfolded the paper to see the result of each cut.

"Did you hear? They're pushing back pathfinder trials until spring," Lucy made conversation while she drew her next pattern. "Apparently, the adaptive training ground will be under repair during the winter." Chandi wondered how much of the repairs had to do with Ryland angling to spend winter at Unseen Waters instead of the ruins of Chicago.

"I'm sorry to hear that—I know you were looking forward to trying out again."

Lucy shrugged. "Nothing to be done about it but wait and keep practicing." She skimmed the pencil over the paper, making a lattice that looked like holly. She stuck the tip of the tongue just past her lips as she concentrated. Chandi kept waiting for Lucy to demand answers, but she remained uncharacteristically disinterested.

"I have the chance to leave," Chandi blurted out. Lucy stopped her pencil in mid-drawing. "If I want. It's up to me. My parents made it a condition of my joining the church. I get to decide if I want to continue when I turn seventeen."

Lucy restarted her doodle where she left off. "Do you want to leave?"

"No!" Chandi swiveled her wedge of paper and made another cut. "Maybe. Sometimes I think about what life could have been if I had stayed with my parents, but other times, I can't imagine my life without the church."

Lucy turned the paper to continue her scroll. "How long have you known?"

"The abbess told me the night before we went on the last tribute visit." Chandi punched out a stubborn piece of paper that didn't want to release.

Lucy brushed off the debris before picking up her piping tube of glue. "And when do you have to decide?"

Chandi changed to a smaller pair of scissors. "Sometime around the new year."

"Is that why you had to leave suddenly?"

"No, that was something else. Someone important was sick and I sat with them until they got better." Chandi had promised to tell Lucy as much as she could, but she didn't think she had the right to share others' secrets, just her own.

"Did they get better?"

"Eventually. They even gave me a gift afterward—a fat shiny pearl! Brother Bartholomew is examining it now, but as soon as he's finished with it, I'll show it to you. What do you think?" Chandi flattened her well-creased sheet of paper and unveiled her snowflake.

Lucy handed her the glue pot. "Needs more sparkle."

Quiet lingered in the room as the roommates worked on their respective crafts. Chandi cursed the more intricate curves she had just cut out now that she was having to outline them with glue. Lucy broke the silence, "Do you think you could be happy if you didn't run? If you didn't have sentients need you and your abilities?

"I could still run and use my abilities outside of the church. It would just be in my own village," Chandi countered.

"But it isn't really the same, is it?" Lucy handed her the shaker. Chandi watched the shimmering confetti slip through the gouged holes. She tried to imagine waking without morning devotion, running without her brothers and sisters of the stride, falling asleep without Lucy's light snore above her—life without the constant hum of activity within the monastery's walls under the vigilant eye of the Order of the Guard.

"No, I suppose it's not," Chandi conceded. "Aren't you mad?"

Lucy shook out glitter over the glue. "Would it help?"

"No, but this quiet Zen thing is freaking me out."

Lucy dusted her holly chain with green bits. "I've known for a long time that we would eventually have to go our separate ways. I think that's part of the reason I was so upset after the last pathfinder trials. Somewhere deep inside, I knew it was the beginning of our paths diverging. I made a decision to enjoy the time we still had rather than dwell on how it was going to end. So yeah, I'm sad, but it's hard to be mad at the inevitable. I'm not pissed at the sun for rising or the rooster for crowing. I'm more concerned that you make a choice that's good for you, and with any luck that decision buys us a little more time together."

Chandi sat dumbstruck. How had she missed so much in the past few months? Was she really so self-centered that she couldn't see what was going on right in front of her, sleeping above her, eating dinner across from her? In that moment, she forgot all about Moonstone and octopoids and her theoretical married-with-children secular life. Big, fat tears pooled in her eyes. "When did you get so wise?"

"Pretty sure it happened last Tuesday," Lucy answered sarcastically before looking up from her work. "Don't you start! If you cry, I'll cry."

"Too late," Chandi sniffled. "I'm sorry you had to go through that alone."

"I wasn't alone. You were there, too. You just didn't know what was happening," Lucy managed to get her words out before blubbering. Together they wept and talked and laughed in a way they hadn't in a very long time. They had no idea where the future would take them, but for now, they had each other.

*****

"You have an x-ray?!" Ryland exclaimed with childlike glee.

"You don't get to be my age without collecting all manner of things," Bartholomew stated prosaically as he perused his books. With a wave of his feathered hand and a puff of his pipe, he gave the tinker his blessing. "If you can get it working, you're more than welcome to use it."

Ryland extricated the small box from a precarious jumble of junk, assessing what seemed salvageable and what needed replacing. He suddenly recalled a crucial fact that he had overlooked in his initial excitement. "There's one problem. It requires radiation."

Bartholomew looked up from his reading and furrowed his brow. "That may not be as big of a problem as you think," the scholar commented, remembering a stash of radioactive material stored in a metal box that they had used to assess and hone Chandi's abilities. If the lead protected sentients from radiation, theoretically it should protect the radioactive material from Chandi's aura. "If you can get the electrics working, I may be able to get my hands on some operational supplies."

"Maybe I could rig it so it wouldn't need radiation…" Ryland speculated as he took off the casing, producing all manner of screwdrivers from thin air until he found the right size.

"You're a tinker; I trust you'll sort it," the scholar brushed off his companion's conjecture and returned to his research. Truth be told, Bartholomew didn't mind Ryland's company; he was a fellow seeker of knowledge, albeit with a different set of tools. It took the owl some time to pick up on Ryland's penchant for talking through problems, but now that he understood that the tinker was mostly talking to himself, they could both get on with their work in convivial company.

Bartholomew was engrossed by Chandi's pearl of making; he could not do nearly as much of an examination with the freshwater pearl he had procured for her birthday…at least, not without getting thoroughly soaked in the process. According to his tomes, natural pearls were very rare, and took years to develop as mollusks deposited layers of nacre on the offending insult in their shell. In time, the ancients invented various methods of cultivating pearls, both in salt water and fresh water environments. The more lustrous cultured pearls started off as a sliver of mantle tissue inserted into the shell, eliciting the mussel to deposit layers of nacre. Alternatively, they could implant a spherical bead, giving the mollusk a mold upon which to secrete layers of iridescent coating. If Ryland could get the x-ray machine working, it would allow Bartholomew to see inside the pearls without destroying them.

Ryland, on the other hand, was more interested in the tech behind the water production. It was obvious that the gray pearl was a finer gem, not only in terms of size, shape, and luster, but also in terms of water output. When thought-activated, it created water at a faster rate, filling a given container exponentially faster than the oblong white pearl. Sadly, neither pearl glowed purple to him, so they weren't absorbable pieces of tech that could be repurposed. There were no parts to fiddle with and no discernable spouts from which water flowed. Without better diagnostic gear, he was at a loss. Which is how he found himself rummaging through Bartholomew's heap of castoffs—things the old bird couldn't get working, but was sure could be of purpose in the right hands.

*****

The blood seeped into the wet snow, coloring the ground a

rich burgundy that faded to a pale pink on its fringes. The orange glow from the burning buildings cast ominous shadows as the victors celebrated their glory. True, the frigid river crossing had claimed more than a few and the battle had been harder than the last, but Brockville succumbed in the end and pillaging renewed their spirits and communal bonds. Cries pierced the night as another pocket of hidden settlers was rooted out.

Terem bit down on the leather strap as the glowing metal seared his flesh, cauterizing the wound he sustained in the fray. Steam rose from the gash as they packed it with fresh clean snow. The pain only fueled his rage. The journey south was not his idea, but if this was what they wanted, so be it.

Another wail floated from the smoke as a sentient ran from the flames, heading for the barren tree line. Terem quickly rifled through the confiscated crates and loaded an en bloc clip in the newly looted M1 Garand. He caught the figure in his sites, making small adjustments each time he fired until he downed his target. A heady cheer rang out from his companions. They were the Laughter at the End of Time. There would be no mercy.

Chapter Twelve

"What's this I hear about you leaving?" Willem inquired as they settled with their bowls of pottage. Chandi rolled her eyes—Lucy may have gotten all centered and wise, but she still couldn't keep a secret.

"It's just an option, so don't count on me going anywhere quite yet," Chandi stated simply.

"Where is Chandi going?" Hanu appeared from around the corner.

"Back to her village," Willem filled him in.

"It's not decided!" Chandi clarified with more force than she intended.

"What's not decided?" Sura asked from the other side as she and Lucy joined them.

"Chandi's leaving the church," Hanu replied.

Chandi glared at Lucy as she stirred her porridge. "I may have mentioned it was a possibility," she casually commented. "They're your friends; they have a right to know."

Willem shook his head vociferously. "Don't be a dumbass! You don't really want to leave the church. It's full of wastelanders and war and starvation out there."

Hanu forehead wrinkled. "You don't know how much it kills me to say this, but I agree with Willem."

"Hey!" Lucy interjected. "It's Chandi's decision and as her friends, we are going to support her in whatever she decides. Even if it is a boneheaded decision."

"Thanks, I think." Chandi wasn't sure if she should be offended or flattered by the brouhaha. "It's not all or nothing. I may be able to stay and keep training and just not have to go on tribute trips. I still have time to think about it."

"At least you have a village to go back to," Sura spat out bitterly as hot tears welled up in her azure eyes. "Excuse me, I'm suddenly not hungry." She ran out of the lunchroom, dropping her bowl off on the way out. Lucy instinctively rose, but Hanu was already standing and placed his hand on her shoulder.

"You finish lunch. I'll find her. If anyone asks, we were running laps with you at the beginning of meditation."
Lucy, taken aback by the uncharacteristic command in Hanu's voice and masterful manner, simply nodded.

He dashed out into the courtyard and pulled his cloak close against the cold. There was no sign of Sura, but he had a hunch and followed his gut into the orchards. He didn't see her among the barren branches, but Hanu knew that didn't necessary mean she wasn't there.

"Sura, it's me. I just wanted to see if you were okay." Hanu waited while the trees' naked limbs rustled in the wind and danced against the gray sky. "You don't have to show yourself, but fair warning, it's either me or Lucy." He was about to turn around and finish his lunch when he heard Sura's small voice from above.

"Wait! I'm up here." Hanu looked up as she blinked into sight, her petite body curled into a ball seven feet up. The fine flaxen wisps that escaped her plait stuck to her tear-streaked face. "How did you know I'd be here?"

Hanu deftly climbed up. "Call it simian intuition. Where else would you go if you wanted to be left alone? No one ever thinks to look up." He opened a pouch of dried fruit and nuts—cold lunch is better than no lunch. He turned the sack toward Sura and her stomach growled in reply.

"I'm so embarrassed," Sura confessed after eating a handful of trail mix.

"I wouldn't let it weigh too heavy on your mind. In that group, you're not even in the running for drama queen. Hands down, Willem's won three years in a row." Hanu caught her smile in the corner of his eye. "You want to talk about it?"

"Not particularly," Sura replied.

"You want a hug?" Hanu spread open his cloak. "Limited time offer, it's windy up here." Sura edged closer and snuggled against his warm fur. He curled his arm around her and rested his hand on her shoulder. She lay her head against his chest; she could hear his heartbeat. Eventually her shivering lessened.

"Do we have to meditate today?" Sura asked with dread.

"Eventually, but not right away. We can pretend we were running laps, but we can't stay up here too long. They'll get wise and Netu might send Umbra to fetch us," Hanu gently joked. Sura shuddered at the thought of the giant arachnid.

*****

Khiri reread the missive one more time. Dexter's request for troop support from the Order of the Guard was an unusual request, an indictment on continuous war and how it drains the lifeblood from the land, but this was not the time to wax philosophic. There were wastelanders running amok in the Kingdom of a Thousand Islands. At the time of Dexter's appeal, the muties had just taken Brockville; the whole of the kingdom was at risk, including the ruins of Watertown.

According to Aren's report, there were one hundred and twenty soldiers currently stationed in the barracks just outside the Monastery of Unseen Waters. The captain of the guard felt confident that they could operate on a skeleton crew of fifty, and send seven squads east to repel the invaders, as long as other precautions were taken to compensate for their reduced presence. Ryland assured the abbess that the plasma gun that killed the groue horror earlier this year was repaired and fully operational.

Ordinarily, she wouldn't entertain such a request; the Order of the Guard was there to serve the Church of Parkour and protect the monastery. Even if she were tempted to send aid, she wasn't in the habit of making unilateral decisions of this magnitude. But time was short and the stakes—as well as the rewards—were high. Dexter was offering nothing short of alienating the land under the monastery and turning it into an allodial holding owned by the Church of Parkour. It seemed an exorbitant gift for seventy warriors, which told Khiri that this was Dexter's last stand. Unlike his other wars, if this campaign failed, there would be no kingdom to preserve, much less grant beneficent holdings. Dexter's message was clear: the survival of his kingdom in exchange for giving the monastery its freedom.

The order was on her desk. All she had to do was sign it and Aren would dispatch the troops. Ariadne would implement the necessary security measures. Their small slice of Watertown would belong to Church of Parkour. With the wave of her wrist, the mother of stride cast their fate.

*****

The fat flurries drifted down, blanketing the ground. Chandi spun underneath, catching snowflakes in her mouth and on her eyelashes. The once verdant green had disappeared under a layer of white, and the clean lines of the groomed hedges were softened by the fluffy snow. She entered and turned right down the narrow passage; she had run the king's maze enough times in fair weather to know the way.

As she rounded the corner, she leapt back—the statue of the lion in repose was now a lion rampant, its rocky form reared up on its hind legs in a fierce pose. Were Chandi not in such a rush, she might have stopped to ponder the change, but she was on a mission. She needed to make it to the center of labyrinth.

The rapidly falling wet snow made each step a labor. She paused to catch her breath at the marbled Greek goddess, hair swept up with tendrils escaping their bondage, one breast exposed with the other draped in delicate folds. Chandi felt the gaze of her blank stony eyes upon her and continued her trek.

Her legs felt like lead, her feet of clay. She didn't have much farther to go, just a few more steps to the center of the maze. Chandi listened for the burbling of its fountain, but heard nothing. It was only when she cleared the last of the hedges that she understood why. Atop the great fount was a giant pearl of making, much larger than Chandi's. Its once-flowing water was frozen in place, its fluid fall captured in clear crystalline arcs.

Chandi reached up for the gem, only to find it progressively more difficult to lift her arm. She looked down and her abdomen was already alabaster, the rigid pallor creeping up her arm. She tried to move her legs but they were fastened to the ground. She felt the gypsum coat her skin, hardening in place. She tried to open her mouth to speak, but found her lips immovable, captured in their neutral pucker. A milky curtain fell over her vision as her green eyes transformed into blank ivory orbs.

Chandi abruptly opened her eyes and her racing heart slowed as they darted back and forth, confirming that she was inside her own room. She shook all four of her limbs under her covers, just to make sure she could. She swore softly. "Moonstone, we have got to teach you to use your words. I'm done with these donked-up dreams."

Chapter Thirteen

Ryland rubbed his hand across his coarse stubble before stroking his patch of facial hair, a sure sign he was ruminating. The abbess had more pressing demands that required his immediate attention, but the x-ray machine was never far from his mind. It was equal parts challenge and entertainment. "Maybe if I take the coil from the toaster…" he muttered to himself as he worked his way through the more mundane monastic repairs.

Scavenged from the remains of a dentist's office in suburban Watertown, the portable x-ray machine had pictorials along its structure, reminders on how to properly operate the machine. Bartholomew gave the tinker access to the technological tomes in his library, but there weren't many, and a few of them even predated the broken moon—the laws that once governed the natural world then no longer applied. That wasn't to say that science and technology didn't adhere to rules under the shattered moon, just different ones.

It was late in the afternoon before the tinker made it back to the scholar's workshop, chopping pieces of other appliances to put into his pet project. Layers of grease and sweat later, Ryland admitted defeat and reluctantly decided he needed more drastic measures. As his mentor elegantly put it, when science wasn't getting the job done, it was time for super science.

Ryland had found more than his fair share of special tech, thanks to his ability to navigate the ruins with relative ease. It could be anything—a pencil sharpener, a combination padlock, an empty disposable lighter—the base item wasn't as important as the fact that it contained nanite programming that only tinkers could see by virtue of their little friends. Where others saw junk, tinkers saw every shade of purple from lavender to puce—how the parts broadcast the type and strength of the tech encapsulated within. These beauties were technological wildcards; as long as Ryland matched the right type of tech at sufficient strength, his nanites could jury-rig the part into the design like it belonged there in the first place.

He carried his motley collection inside him, using his nanites to absorb the item's programming into his body for safekeeping. The only problem was that his memory wasn't what it used to be, and it sometimes took time to hunt down the right part. He cleared a corner and started spontaneously materializing items from his hands: not the burr grinder, not the hex key, not the analog watch face, not the kite string, not the theracane—*ah ha!*—the garlic press! It glowed a soft magenta in his hands. He set it aside and reabsorbed the rest of his cache—a place for everything and everything in its place.

Ryland was parsimonious with using these special parts; when you repurposed it, you essentially altered the programming for a specific purpose and its malleability was spent. He positioned the garlic press and got to work, fondly remembering the first time he had seen such a feat—how was *that* going to fit in *there*?

Ryland was tightening the last screw when Bartholomew returned from his meeting. The tinker wiped off his hands and flipped the switch. The red light on the side turned on. "I believe we are in need of some operational supplies."

*****

"You two are having way too much fun," Chandi remarked as she entered Bartholomew's study. She was pretty certain they had x-rayed everything in the room before she had arrived to pick up her pearls. "Are you sure that thing is safe to use? Last time I checked, skull and crossbones were bad and radiation is poison."

"This machine uses low energy, and I've made a lead shield to stand behind while it's in use," Ryland reassured her.

"And you were never far away," Bartholomew obliquely referred to her ability to clear nearby radiation, adding, "I'm just glad this stuff still works," as he patted the canister. "Come look at this." He motioned to the screen.

Chandi squinted at the soft, fuzzy black and white image.

"What am I looking at?"

"Your pearls!" the scholar exclaimed, as if it was obvious. "This spherical one is the gray pearl of making, while this oblong one is the one I gave you. I had to contain it for obvious reasons, but the resolution couldn't be more telling." Chandi nodded, humoring her brothers of the stride.

"Neither pearl is natural, but they are products of completely different processes." Bartholomew's strigiform face lit up with the implications. "See this curved slither? That's a small piece of mantle inserted into the mussel to simulate pearl production. It's a different composition from the actual layers of nacre. Now look at this one." He guided her attention with a wave of his hand. "See the faint black circle within the sphere? That's a bead they used so the mollusks have something to coat with nacre. Thus the spherical shape."

Chandi perked up. "Wait, so you're saying that if you stick something into one of these clams—"

"Mollusks, more generally, but specific pearl-producing mussels or oysters depending on the water and climate," the scholar corrected her.

"Right, so if you stick something into one of these nacre-secreting bivalves, they will coat it until it becomes a pearl?" Bartholomew took a puff of his pipe and nodded. "Can this machine tell us anything about what the bead is?"

"No, it just captures the level of radiation absorbed by the materials. The difference in composition is what renders a black and white picture," Ryland explained.

"If you really wanted to know more about the seeding material, hypothetically, a weak acid solution might work," the scholar conjectured. "I read somewhere that a simple vinegar bath could dissolve the nacre of mundane pearls, but there is no way of telling if that would work with these pearls without destroying them."

"Which I was told was off limits," Ryland rambunctiously interjected. Chandi gave him a sour look.

"So where does the water production come into this? Presumably not all pearls make water."

Ryland fielded this question. "Not sure. Tinkering is mostly screwing about with stuff that's broken, or cobbling together parts and pieces to see what you can make. There isn't much for me to work with since I'm not allowed to damage the goods, but my best guess is that tech is being infused in the process of making of pearls themselves."

"Wait, nanite-infused nacre? Are we talking about a mechanical oyster?" Chandi speculated.

Ryland grinned. "Creepy, eh?"

"So what would happen if someone put something otherworldly in our academic mech bivalve?" Chandi asked.

The very notion of sorcery and technology co-mingling caused Bartholomew to inhale too sharply from his pipe and cough uncontrollably. Ryland cast an inquisitive glare at the pathfinder as she fetched a glass of water for the old bird.

Chandi shook her head at the tinker while she held the cup to Bartholomew's lips. The question was left dangling in the commotion and once that died down, Chandi slipped out of the room with her two pearls. Their respective reaction was confirmation of her gut instinct—science and sorcery did not play well together. As she wove through the hallways of the monastery, she set aside her concerns. She had other things to attend to tonight; Moonstone was going to have to wait.

Ryland helped Bartholomew put everything away—even with containment, since no one wanted to sleep next to a canister of radioactive material. "Now that you're got that fixed, what's your next project?" Bartholomew nudged the tinker in hopes of getting more usable equipment.

Ryland eyed the pile in the basement and considered the abbess's string of requests. "Oh, I'm sure I'll find something to occupy my hands." As they parted ways, Ryland suddenly realized how famished he was—he had worked straight through dinner. He headed to the kitchen in hopes of a late-night snack and rustled up some bread, cheese, and an apple. As he returned to his room, he walked past a bank of windows and caught sight of some students sneaking out into the snowfall. *Ah, to be young.* He grinned between morsels of food.

*****

"What are we doing out here, Chandi? It's cold!" Sura

whined softly.

"I don't have the faintest clue," Chandi categorically rejected culpability. "Lucy told me to bring you here. I'm just following orders." Chandi hoisted open the door to one of the work sheds and indicated Sura should enter.

The room was flooded with candlelight that caught the glint of the glitter and splashes of color that dangled all around. Chandi quickly shut out the cold wind before it could extinguish the flames. Sura awed at the paper icicles and snowflakes suspended from the low rafters, and it took her a second to realize they weren't alone as Lucy emerged from behind a pillar, pinning a garland held up by Willem that spiraled around the stout beam. Hanu was also there, holding a jug of freshly purloined milk from a rather cranky cow.

"What is all this?" Sura wondered.

"None of us have really done Christmas before, but I know you used to back home, so we thought we'd bring Christmas to you this year," Lucy explained through her mouth full of tacks. "We couldn't really cut down a tree without the rest of the monastery noticing and it's way too cold and windy to light a tree out there, so I hope this festive structural support will do."

"I brought cookies," Chandi interjected as she unfolded a scarf of lavender shortbread from her inner pocket.

"Thanks to Millie, we have fresh milk," Hanu declared victoriously. "That's what you put out for Santa, right? Milk and cookies?" Sura nodded and Hanu looked relieved to have gotten it right.

"And Willem was just about to nail up our socks and put fruit and nuts in them," Lucy added cheerfully. It sounded absurd to her, but according to what Chandi had read in a book, it was tradition.

"You don't need to put a hole in perfectly good socks," Sura stopped him before he started hammering. "Stockings are socks that have loops on the end *designed* for hanging," she tactfully explained. Willem shrugged and grabbed a cookie instead.

"And we have extra ornaments to hang on the pillar!"

"Where did you get all these?" Sura marveled at the bits and bobs on hooks.

"They're technically for Longest Night, so try to act surprised when you see them next week," Chandi muttered conspiratorially and handed her a cookie before they were all eaten. "See that snowflake?" she pointed to the far corner. "I did that one," she crowed with pride.

Sura suddenly got very quiet and embarrassed. "I don't know what to say."

"I say we eat up and go make snow angels," Lucy recommended, sparing Sura from having to make a speech.

"Or snowmen," Willem backed her up.

Chandi was about to object that she just got in from the cold when Lucy caught her arm. "Hanu, don't forget to give Sura her Christmas present before you come out," she yelled over her shoulder as she pulled Chandi back into the cold.

Hanu placed the jug on the ground and fished out a small package from his pocket. He held it out in Sura's general direction. It was wrapped in a parchment paper with a bright red ribbon tied around it. "Go on. It's from all of us." He watched Sura open it with care, cradling the gift in its wrapping paper. She gasped in shock at the sight of the polished silver trinity knot.

The bewildered Sura finally found her voice. "Where did you find this?"

"It was in your box. We all have a box of our things from before we joined the church, stashed away in storage. Lucy has a knack for getting into places she shouldn't be and 'liberating' items," Hanu explained.

Sura reverently traced its unending lines with her finger. "My father made it. One for me and one for my sister. I thought I had lost it." She closed her hands around it and wrapped her arms tightly around Hanu. "Thank you."

Hanu found it impossible not to hug her back. "Don't get too excited. No doubt Lucy knows when your birthday is now."

"That's okay. It was last month."

"That just gives her eleven months to plan for your fifteenth birthday." Sura laughed and they awkwardly let go of each other. "Hey, are snowball fights a Christmas tradition?"

Sura nodded emphatically. "Most definitely."

Chapter Fourteen

If Halldix had his druthers, he would have stayed the winter in Oswego. On the fringe of the Lordship of Fingers's territory, it was blissfully unencumbered by the "octopoid way" and the tinker was at liberty to discover and create. Before the complaints of spirit activity in the area by the vertebrate that lived there, Halldix had conducted his research and inventions in Rochester along the shores of Lake Ontario, home to the breeding chambers that filled the ranks of their militia and pumped out freshwater pearls for trade and pearls of making for themselves. It wasn't until he got to Oswego that he realized how much he had to learn.

Out on the frontier, disengaged from the stifling social restraints and political machinations of the noble families, Halldix did the unthinkable—he went into the ruins. It didn't take long for him to realize the potential buried among the ancients' rubble. He didn't bother to ask why his people were not capitalizing on this resource, because he already knew the answer. It was unoctopoid.

He did his best to make use of the humans that remained

in the Lordship of Fingers's stable, but most were young and inexperienced. After the annexation of Oswego from the Kingdom of a Thousand Islands, many sorcerers did not take kindly to their tentacled masters and fled, while the oldest of them simply committed suicide upon capture, choosing rebirth from the otherworld if they had already perfected their spells under the shattered moon. After a close encounter with a two-headed spectral beast that breathed fire and noxious gas, Halldix finally convinced his uncle of the gravity of the situation and gained permission to parlay with the Church of Parkour.

He was surprised how civil the envoy was; all his life, he had heard tales of the wicked and heartless ways of the vertebrates—they hunted and ate octopoid children!—and how the ban against the Church of Parkour was there to protect the octopoids from exploitation. Halldix marveled at the ease and confidence with which they entered the ruins and set up camp, how their sorcerers tamed the spirits, and how their healer took the sickness from him that crushed herbs and a dozen leeches couldn't.

But staying was out of the question; when His Tentacled Majesty Droxithal Purammon summoned you by name, there was no choice but to comply. It was his duty to return to Syracuse, not just to his uncle but to the kingdom. Rumors of Purammon's diminished vigor had reached Halldix's ears, and each year, more nobles speculated if this was the year of his mating.

All octopoids were orphans by nature; adults died shortly after spawning. That was the octopoid way—la petit mort precedes the big death. When Halldix proposed turning his research to prolonging octopoid life after coitus, his uncle dismissed it as a foolish enterprise. "The last thing we need are a bunch of old octopoids grousing about how the young are doing everything wrong. Better to live your life, breed, and die."

At the time, Halldix's objection was practical—imagine how they could advance if knowledge could be passed down generationally, if the young had the benefit of their parents' wisdom in their youth It wasn't until recently that Halldix objected on a moral level, watching the vertebrates with their young. Now, it struck him as especially cruel all the way around.

However, his uncle had a point. As Halldix learned more about the history of the ancients, he discovered an alarming propensity for usurpation when the next generation was ready to seize control of their fate. When his uncle finally answered the call of his hectocotylus, Halldix would become regent. He would have his time to steer the Lordship of Fingers in a more progressive direction until one of Purammon's brood proved themselves worthy of the throne. Purammon's children would not need to resort to patricide to rule.

Halldix peered out from his palanquin at the flowing river; it hadn't frozen yet. Were he in better health and not encumbered with supplies, he would have preferred to travel via the river and feel the velvety water against his skin. Alas, that was the nature of duty: to do what was required of you. If you lived a virtuous life, duty was not too heavy of a burden but your personal desires were sometimes its blood price.

As Onondaga Lake's drain neared, Halldix steeled himself for what awaited him outside Syracuse: an aging king and uncle, a swarm of nobles vying to give him counsel, and an endless stream of assemblies, congresses, and social engagements. He purified his three hearts so none could accuse them of not beating true.

*****

The council members were all in their seats well before the prayer wheel was spun, eager to start and be done with the last meeting of the year. After the grueling ordeal of hammering out the budget, everyone was ready for a rest. Today's meeting should be brief: settle outstanding business so they could start fresh in the new year. How could they have known a missive from the abbess of Unseen Waters was steadily making its way toward them? How could the abbess have known her letter would arrive to a barebones administrative staff while the rest of the church elders took extended time off to celebrate the Longest Night? As far as the agenda was concerned, there were no new requests to consider.

Cassie found the smoke from the incense particularly pungent today, and judging from the subtle coughs of other attendees, she was not the only one who found it so. She took the prescribed moment of silence as the prayer wheel rattled down to center herself. *Remember, it's all in how you sell it.*

The senior steward called the meeting to order, and Cassie rose to speak. "Esteemed councilmen and women, I bring news from our efforts to open relations with the Lordship of Fingers. We had a successful dialogue in Oswego with their representative, Lord Halldix Kepoi. He was most appreciative of our assistance in the otherworldly infestation that was plaguing the nearby settlement and in the process, I retrieved a number of unique spirits that will ignite a new phase in our research and development. Additionally, I have laid the foundation for future communication in the new year."

The sorcerer took her seat, waiting for comment and questions. "The octopoids have a reputation for being highly xenophobic. How did you find them in Oswego?"

"His lordship seemed most pleased in our cultural exchange. Oswego, as a former holding of the Kingdom of a Thousand Islands, is one of few areas where octopoids are in contact with vertebrates, as they call us. There are still substantial gaps in knowledge between them, but exposure is a promising start."

"You spoke of spirit retrieval, but what of the rock deposited there. Was that recovered?"

"Despite our extensive search, we were unable to locate

Moonstone. We have every reason to believe that this will not be the only official visit the Church of Parkour makes to Oswego, and have an action plan for further exploration."

"Further exploration? I thought you said the initial search was extensive?"

Cassie mentally told Councilman Pollack to eat a bag of dicks but maintained her composure and neutral mien. "Our initial search was limited to land, but our future pursuits will include aquatic terrain. The area experienced significant flooding in the fall and it would be short-sighted to *not* expand our perimeters."

"How can you be so sure the octopoids will have you back?" Councilwoman Ratch was as perceptive as she was keen.

"Without getting too technical, a disposable device was planted in Oswego that will slowly expose the area to spirit activity once winter passes. Furthermore, Lord Kepoi was informed that the spirit problem, while improved, would require ongoing attention. I took the liberty of extending the Church of Parkour's assistance to His Tentacled Majesty in the future." The elders stared dumbstruck at Cassie's revelation, but the sorcerer didn't flinch.

There were a handful of axioms that guided Cassie through the machinations of the elder council: you get more flies with honey than vinegar, it's better to ask forgiveness than permission, and the supreme art of war is to subdue the enemy without fighting.

"Throughout this assignment, it has come to my attention that there are significant lapses in our understanding of the octopoids. However, I have located a tracer who has personal experience with 'the eight-limbed' who is currently at Unseen Waters. With your permission, I would like to spend some time at the monastery to update our knowledge in anticipation of future relations." There was no petition in her request despite the optics of supplication.

Councilman Luther cracked a small smirk. "Where you choose to celebrate Longest Night is none of our concern, as long as you are back to work in time for the next meeting."

*****

War has a way of letting you know who your friends are. Who will fight to the end by your side and who will flee, who will answer the call for aid and who will meekly find any excuse to sit this one out. After news of the fall of Brockville, His Royal Highness, King Dexter Albert Winchester VI called in all his favors. All his nobles came with their retinues to defend their kingdom from the unrelenting destruction the wastelanders brought. The Oswald brother sent scouts and four squads of rangers well accustomed to wilderness combat. The seven squads of the Order of the Guard came disciplined, armed, and armored. If a man could measure his worth by his allies, Dexter had lived a good life.

A lifetime of war gave him piercing insight: how long would it take for each of his allies to join his force, how quickly the wastelanders could move and their most likely path, and where and when they should take their stand. If he waited, he could amass more troops, but then more of his kingdom would be subject to the parasitic hunger and destruction of the invaders from the north.

The trap was set along a stretch of road just north of Gouvernear, the next logical target for an invading force marching on their stomachs. Dexter knew the terrain well and selected a slightly hilly bend in the road to set up their ambush. He positioned his forces on either side of the valley, mounding the snow into a bank to conceal the soldiers from the road. When Dexter gave the signal, a rain of fire would descend on them from high ground on both sides while engagement troops in front and back would stop their retreat. Drawing the enemy in and attacking their flank was an old tactic, elegantly lethal in its simplicity.

According to the scouts' recon, the wastelanders were six hundred strong and should arrive in late afternoon. Dexter would lead half of the soldiers on one side of the valley road, with his son-in-law Stephen leading the other half. After forming the snow banks, the soldiers took their positions while the rangers brushed away any tracks in the snow visible from the north. That familiar tension before battle coiled in Dexter's gut, like a spring waiting to be sprung.

As the sun lowered toward the horizon, a falcon soared in the sky. "You'll have a feast if you can just be patient," Dexter told the hunter. An altogether different birdcall came from up ahead—they were coming. The seconds stretched but the forces held their discipline and nerve. Dexter was well acquainted with the temporal tautness, but timing was crucial. Spring the trap too soon and you lose your advantage. Wait too long and you risk letting enemy forces escape…or worse, attack your lines from the flank or rear.

A stillness settled in Dexter's tight throat. It was time. He gave the signal and a chorus of sharp shrills echoed in the valley. The gunners rose and fired upon the unaware muties; a line of pikemen speared any that tried to rush the hill while they reloaded. Spiked barricades were placed at the beginning and end of the column and reinforced with infantry, making it harder for the invaders to escape Dexter's trap.

There was a unity of purpose among Dexter's army; they attacked for their friends and families, for the homes they created, for the life they had scratched out of the earth under the shattered moon. They fought for everything they had built so that it was not created in vain; otherwise, nothing mattered. Wastelanders were everyone's problem; with them, there was no negotiation, no reconciliation, no mercy. Wherever muties went, there was only carnage and loss.

The ambush was masterfully executed and Dexter, now astride his steed, kept his eyes on the ebb and flow of bodies, looking for weak spots in the line that needed reinforcing. There were small gaps where wastelanders had made a successful charge up the hill, but Dexter's and Stephen's lines were intact. The northeast side took heavy losses until the southeast gunners took out muties armed with semi-automatic weapons. They tightened ranks so the enemy could not split them, and Dexter sent cavalry to bolster the end of the line.

Suddenly Dexter's mount reared as a loud explosion shook the ground, throwing up snow, flesh, and dirt. The front barricade and many of the infantrymen were torn to bits by a grenade. Like a hole in a dam, a gush of invaders flowed out of the valley—some fleeing, others taking out their vengeance on the front of Stephen's line from the flank. Dexter drove his horse to the other side of the road, running down as many as he could in the process, and rallied those who survived the blast. He took down five with Lucille, his trusty Colt Paterson, before its bullets were spent and he drew his sword.

Dexter let loose a battle cry and a grim smile came over his face. The blood coursed through his veins and once again, he enjoyed the thrust of hand-to-hand combat—he never felt more alive than in contest. There was no order here, just each sentient fighting for their life. The Order of the Guard switched to melee weapons and entered the fray alongside the pikemen and infantry. Stephen stood among them, boosting morale and leading the defense.

Dexter led his regrouped squad into the brawl, hacking

his way through foe until he met friend. A rebar tip stung deep into the flank of his horse, causing it to buck and throw its master from its back before falling on its side in agony. Dexter found his feet and whipped his sword into his horse's attacker—that was his favorite mare! The steel sliced deep into the wastelander's thigh, severing her femoral vein and staining the dirty snow a deep crimson.

Dexter slogged his way to his son-in-law and they fought to re-establish the line. They parried swords, deflected spears, evaded clubs and axes, and blocked fists, claws, and toothy maws. As the fighting wound down and the gunfire petered out, the final tally became clear: Dexter's troops stood in a swath of the fallen.

Stephen organized the soldiers into the post-combat routine familiar to all battlefields since the dawn of time: distinguishing the wounded from the dead, mercy killing those who were grievously injured, looting corpses, recovering weapons and ammunition, and setting up camp for the night. Dexter cleaned off his blade and took a seat against a nearby tree. He had seen many a battlefield in his time, but never one this close to home. Less than a day's ride on a fast horse was his estate, where his daughter waited, expecting her first child—his grandchild. Only now, after the fighting was complete, did he allow himself to think about Emma.

He consoled himself with the thought that all this would be gone in the spring: the blood, the gore, the snow. The hillside would bloom with clover like it did every summer, and no one would know what transpired here. *War does not determine who is right, only who is left.* Dexter read that somewhere once, or maybe his father had and told him about it—he was the more avid reader of the two. Dexter was more a man of action, but at this very moment, he was bone-tired. He knew he should get his injuries checked, but the medics had more serious wounds to tend and the thought of getting up from his seat against the tree was exhausting. *I have time*, he told himself as he watched the falling snow slowly dust the battlefield white.

Later, when Stephen found Dexter, he merely thought he was sleeping; his face was so serene and peaceful. It wasn't until he tried to rouse him that he knew something was wrong. There was no pool of blood on the ground and when they laid out the body, they could find no lethal wound. Stephen assumed Dexter's heart had given out after the strain of combat. When announced to her, Emma found a measure of solace that her father had died doing what he loved, and she vowed to tell her unborn child their grandfather, King Dexter Albert Winchester VI, died protecting his kingdom.

Chapter Fifteen

The Monastery of Unseen Waters had been on tight security since Aren dispatched the bulk of the Order of the Guard to the Kingdom of a Thousand Islands. More sentries were posted on the wall around the clock and routine ruin inspections were suspended. The abbess halted all visitor traffic in and out of the monastery, both because of the dangers on the road and the fact that she couldn't spare any of the Order of the Guard to accompany travelers. Pathfinder and tracer training were limited to the adaptable training ground, Ryland's focus was shifted to repairing and restoring combat-oriented tech, and Jackson was high alert. Aren wasn't exactly sure what that meant in otherworldly terms, but he had sent the sorcerer out with his soldiers enough times to know that for all his bullshit and bluster, he was pulling his weight keeping the monastery safe.

Aren wasn't a religious sentient by nature, but he burned incense each day his soldiers were gone, just in case there was a higher being that was bestowing favors. The hoofed captain stamped the ground twice in glee as a guard reported sighting a

Church of Parkour carriage approaching the monastery in the company of at least a squad of soldiers. Aren would take all the help he could get.

Unaware of the state of affairs in the Kingdom of a Thousand Islands, Cassie stepped out of the vehicle to a stronger show of force than she was accustomed to. Aren did his best to welcome their visitor, but could not draw her attention away from the fact that the Order of the Guard swiftly closed the monastery gates behind her, nor could she ignore how quickly her escort guards were conscripted into service by the local order.

"Cassie, what are you doing here?" Khiri dropped all trace of neutral formality as soon as she saw her old friend enter her office. "Not that I'm displeased to see you, but it's a dangerous time to be traveling in these parts."

"Officially, I'm here to speak to Ryland, but in all honestly, I really needed a break from politics and wanted to come home for Longest Night." Cassie rose on her tiptoes to embrace the abbess. "What on earth is going on, Khiri? I thought Aren was going to yodel when I showed up with my guards."

"That's speciest," Khiri admonished her with a sly smirk, happy to have a moment to make a joke. "Not all sentients with mountain goats linage yodel…just the good ones, preferably in lederhosen." The abbess motioned for the sorcerer to take a seat. "Did the council not get my letter?" Cassie's befuddled face answered her question. "Wastelanders crossed the Saint Lawrence River and decimated Brockville six days ago. Dexter is marshaling troops to repel them. We sent seven squads to the cause, but we still haven't heard any word from them."

"Seven squads?!" Cassie squawked.

"He was offering to make our portion of Watertown a freehold of the church in exchange. Say what you will about Dexter, he's generous with his friends."

Cassie took off her outer robes and gloves before falling into her chair in disbelief. "And you have this in writing?"

"Of course!" Khiri retorted. "There wasn't time to consult the elder council before making a decision, but I sent them a letter the same day to explain the situation. I was hoping they would send reinforcements to the monastery, in case...." The tigress didn't want to say the words and tempt fate. "But if you're here, I guess that is not going to happen."

"They are all on break for Longest Night." Cassie grimaced. She hated to be the bearer of bad news. "I left right after the last meeting of the year. If you're lucky, someone will recognize the importance of your communication and get it moving through the chain to someone who can do something. Worst case, it will pile up with the other correspondences that won't even be looked at until after Longest Night."

The abbess sighed. "Do you have any good news?"

"I brought bubbly, candied fruit, and nuts?" Cassie attempted levity.

"Let's not pop the cork just yet."

Rumor ran amok within the monastery's walls. The monastery was on high alert and all the adults were nervous; the fact that they weren't telling students made it more ominous. But lack of knowledge didn't stop the creative and curious from speculating. Perhaps a battle was nearby? It was a well-known fact that the Kingdom of a Thousand Islands was at war with everyone. Those that knew about the tribute carriage attack spun tales of rogue bandits and highwaymen. Some were still morbidly fascinated by the slain groue horror, and theorized that something lurked in the ruins of Watertown. The appearance of a second sorcerer at the monastery fueled conjectures that the disturbance was otherworldly in nature. Those that inadvertently guessed upon the truth of the matter were hardly believed. Wastelanders? In this area?

The instructors knew better, briefed early on by the abbess on the nature of the threat. She tasked them with creating an action plan, should the defense of Unseen Waters exceed the capability of the Order of the Guard. All agreed that the younger students need not be informed until it came down to the wire, but tracers should be alerted. After all, they'd signed up to go where they were needed. However, there was some disagreement with what to do with the tracers-in-training.

"Clearly, the tracers-in-training should be told," Netu reasoned. "They are far enough along in their study to be of use should the need arise."

"And what 'use' is that? Combat? That is not what they—or we—are trained to do," Lars objected.

"If it comes down to who survives—us or them—then you better believe I'm joinin' the fight, stillness or not," Bibi declared emphatically.

"While it is not strictly canon, there is a place for offensive maneuvers in Applied Tenets of Faith," Dendra observed after some thought. "Are we not teachers in control of our curriculum?"

"Exactly!" Netu picked up on the gist of her argument. "We are simply advancing their practice to defend themselves against more aggressive attackers."

"By teaching them to fight?" Lars questioned dubiously.

"My daddy always said the best defense is a good offense," Bibi commented. "At least, that's how we do it in the Republic of Texas."

"So what's the plan? If the wastelanders come, we all fight? Who's left to instruct the next generation of runners?" Lars inquired.

"If the wastelanders get inside this monastery, there will be no next generation of runner," Dendra replied. A grim silence hung over the room.

"We have to tell the tracers-in-training what they are up against. They aren't tracers yet; they haven't taken an oath to go where they are needed. They should get to decide for themselves if they fight," Netu reiterated his initial assertion.

"So that's the plan—the four of us, the tracers in residence, and the tracers-in-training fight muties while the pathfinders-in-training secure the novices and tenderfoots?" Bibi put forth for consensus. All four instructors nodded in agreement. "Then I'll inform the abbess that we have a worst-case contingency." She put her hand on Lars's shoulder on her way out. "It's fine to hope for the best, but you also gotta prepare for the worst."

"Did your daddy used to say that, too?" Lars mumbled gruffly.

"No, that was my mamma. Daddy was tough and brave, but she was the wise one."

*****

"I'm not sure if you follow trouble or if trouble follows you," Ryland jeered as he barged into Cassie's room and gave her a hug. "How you are feeling?"

"Better, but I came here for some R&R. I really know how to pick 'em, don't I?" Cassie stuck out her tongue and blew raspberries. "You know where Jackson is? I stopped by his room and no one was there."

Ryland took a seat and decided to keep her company as she finished unpacking. "Probably doing rounds with the Order of the Guard. He's been working day and night ever since the abbess told us about the wastelanders—you know what a sore sport that is for him." Cassie nodded. Having your family butchered by barbarians was rough on any sentient, but even more so for sorcerers. Hearing pleas from the otherworld was heartbreaking when it was your own family's voices ringing in your ears.

Cassie stared off into nowhere and bit the right edge of her lower lip. "I'll check in on him later. He'll get himself killed burning the candle at both ends and getting in a fight." Ryland raised both brows. "What?!"

"Nothing," Ryland replied casually and changed the subject. "I have an academic question to ask you. Theoretically, what would happen if a sorcerous item was imbued with technology?"

Cassie stopped unpacking. "Why do you ask?"

"Something Chandi said a while back," he replied dismissively. "But it got me thinking. I've never heard of anything like that."

She took a seat on her bed. "Well, that's because only a crazy person would do it. Namely wizards—they are the only ones with sorcerous abilities that would tinker with technology."

"But what if a tinker picked up a sorcerous object and incorporated technology?"

Cassie shrugged and resumed emptying her case. "I suppose it's possible, but to what end? It's not like they could work out the sorcerous bit on their own."

"Maybe to no end. I mean, if you aren't a sorcerer, how are

you going know what's enchanted unless someone tells you?" Ryland conjectured. "You and Jackson get the heebie-jeebies whenever you get too close to tech or nanites, but I don't even get an itch on my ass if I'm around otherworldly stuff."

"Eloquent as ever, Ry." Cassie rolled her eyes.

He grinned smugly. "I try."

"It's my turn to ask the questions." She pulled out a pencil and notebook. "I need you to tell me everything you know about octopoids."

Ryland closed his eyes and stroked his facial hair. "Can you be a little more specific?"

Cassie blinked twice. "That was me being specific."

*****

Chandi was starting to lose feeling in her arms as she held the banner's edge above her head. Lucy stood ten feet back, using her fingers and thumbs as a frame for the dangling centerpiece. "A little bit lower on your side, Willem."

He moved his end a few inches lower. "How about here?"

"No, that's too much. Split the difference," Lucy directed.

Willem corrected slowly. "Just tell me when." Chandi admired how level he kept his tone despite the exasperation he must be experiencing.

"There!" Lucy exclaimed. "It's perfect. Nail it down." The redhead moved onto another section of the dining hall where other volunteers were hanging wreaths, garlands, and ornaments. Judging from her tone, they were doing it all wrong.

"I'm beginning to think we got off lightly," Chandi joked as she shook the blood back down to her fingertips.

"Are you sure?" Willem asked rhetorically, "She's my girlfriend, and your roommate and best friend. They only have to hang her decorations once a year."

Chandi gave him an inquisitive stare. "Does Lucy know she's your girlfriend?"

"Well, it's not official, but I've been hinting and she seems keen. At least, she hasn't bothered to correct me," he admitted sheepishly. "I was actually going to ask your opinion on something…." Willem pulled Chandi aside and dug into his pockets. "I found this in the ruins a few weeks ago and never turned it in. I thought it would make a nice gift for Longest Night."

Chandi examined the ivory cameo he placed in her hands. The figure was ethereal, with flowers inserted in her swept-up hair that left her neck and shoulders bare. The vibrant apricot background made her complexion even creamier. The delicate scrollwork around the oval had a black patina, giving the figure even more mystery.

"It's a locket, too. The clasp is on the side," Willem whispered, looking over his shoulder to see if Lucy was looking their way. Chandi fingered a catch, releasing the front to an empty inner chamber. "I haven't figured out if I should put anything in there." Chandi rubbed her fingers gently over the lone curl that softly spilled from the center of her coiffure, feeling its fine detail. "Well, do you think she'll like it?"

"Oh, Willem…" Chandi sighed.

"I knew it!" Willem exclaimed in a hushed tone. "It's too girly for her, isn't it? I should have gotten her something practical. Maybe it's not too late to get her something else—"

"She'll love it, and I happen to know where you can get a chain to match." Chandi placed the cameo carefully in his palm and called loudly over her shoulder. "Lucy, I think we left another box of ornaments in the shed. Willem and I are going to go get it." Lucy acknowledged the yell with a nod before returning her attention to hanging paper icicles and snowflakes.

Willem followed silently behind Chandi as she led him to the basement, the dark dingy domain of spare parts, storage, and damp. It was also where they sorted finds from ruin runs before grading and evaluation. Chandi pulled out a hairpin from her braid and jimmied the lock with ease. She could see fine in low light, but it took Willem's eyes time to adjust.

"How do you know how to do that so well?" Willem broke the silence.

"Who do you think showed Lucy how to get in?" Chandi's green eyes sparked mischievously. She wove her way to the bins of small scrap metal and started sifting, looking for a chain with a working clasp that was the right color and length.

"We are going to get in so much trouble," Willem stated with dread.

"Only if we get caught, so be quiet," Chandi whispered.

"Aren't they going to notice something is missing?" Willem deliberately kept his voice low.

"Do you know how many chains they find in the ruins? I bet most of these are going to be melted down and repurposed."

Willem had a sudden pang of conscious. "Isn't this stealing?"

Chandi's brow knitted in confusion. "You're the one who didn't turn in the locket to begin with."

"But that was an act of omission. This is breaking in and taking something."

"The end result and intent are the same," Chandi scoffed. A satisfied smile broke across her face. "There! Should be a match with a little elbow grease, and it will hang just right."

Chapter Sixteen

The rhythmic beat of the horses' hooves echoed into the night and alerted the sentry on the wall. The rider waved a flag: the Kingdom of a Thousand Islands. Aren sent word to the abbess despite the late hour. No one sends a lone messenger into the night under the shattered moon without it being urgent.

Khiri arrived at the front gate just in time to see the captain of the guard firmly rebuffed. "I was given strict instructions to deliver this message into the abbess's hands directly."

"And now you can fulfill your word." Khiri bowed and rose to her full height after speaking. Her reflective eyes zeroed in on the rider. "May I?" He shrank in his saddle at the quiet authority the mother of the stride projected and relinquished his package. "You must be tired from your ride. You'll find plenty of food and a free bed with the Order of the Guard for the night," she spoke, before retreating to better light and more privacy.

Khiri quickly grasped its gist and releasing her breath. "The wastelanders were defeated just outside Gouvernear by the combined forces," she announced aloud, knowing that Aren wasn't far behind. "There were some causalities and injured among the order, but the bulk of our troop should return in three days' time." The captain clapped his hands and stomped his hooved feet, but stopped himself from outright hugging the abbess. "Yes, good news indeed," she agreed, maintaining her composure, "but we will maintain precautions until we are at full strength, to be on the safe side."

The abbess returned to her office instead of her quarters, poured herself a glass of brandy, and re-read the rest of the message carefully.

Regrettably, the defending force sustained losses, including His Royal Highness, King Dexter Albert Winchester VI. He gave his all for his kingdom. In this time of mourning and transition, I want to reassure the mother of the stride that the Kingdom of a Thousand Islands stands by its allies and honors the close and historic ties it has with the Church of Parkour.

With best regards,

Her Royal Highness, Amelia Marie Winchester Montague

Khiri toasted her fallen contemporary, his last hurrah, and his daughter who had come into her own.

*****

"Who's there? Show yourself!" Jackson commanded the shadows.

"It's just me, Chandi," she hollered out as she sat up. "I'd say 'don't shoot,' but I know you don't carry a gun."

"I do use a crossbow, you know," he retorted. "What are *you* doing out here at this time of night? It's freezing," Jackson scolded her, sounding more like a grumpy old man than he cared to admit.

"I'm staring at the moon," she answered simply. "And the wind isn't bad over here." She motioned.

"Won't you get enough of that tomorrow night?" He took a seat next to her by the tree.

"Tonight is the full moon. Tomorrow, it will be just a little smaller. Plus, the Longest Night isn't about the moon. It's about the sun, and the fact that the tables are finally turning against the night," she stated matter-of-factly. "What are you doing out here? I'm not sitting in the middle of a spirit party, am I?"

"Couldn't sleep, so I offered to help patrol," he grunted. "So what's with you and the moon?"

"I was born during a full moon; at least, that's what my mom use to tell me, so I come out here every full moon. Somewhere out there, she's starting at it, too," Chandi spoke dreamily before snapping out of it. "Sounds really sappy when

I say it out loud."

"It sounds sweet," Jackson reassured her, "and there is nothing wrong with that."

"Jackson, it's messed up that I could understand you and Cassandra talk about Moonstone, isn't it?" It wasn't so much a question as asking for confirmation of a hunch.

"Yeah, it's pretty weird." Jackson never was one to sugarcoat things.

"So what am I supposed to do with that?!" Chandi exasperatedly exclaimed. Jackson didn't have any answers for her. Despite the numerous times Chandi had churned the same things in her mind, no clear path revealed itself. Was she part sorcerer now…was that even a thing? Was it all a fluke, that she was the first person to find it when it fell from the sky? Or was Moonstone looking specifically for her? Was she supposed to help it, or capture and contain it so it couldn't do any more harm? Why couldn't she just wash her hands of all of it and just run?

She was so tired to feeling that way and spoke frankly, in a deflated tone, "I feel like no matter what I do or don't do, I'm going to let someone down or someone is going to get hurt. I wish I could just do my own thing."

Jackson was intimately familiar with the desire to surrender to the void, but he also knew he was terrible at pep talks, so he kept his comments brief. "Everyone thinks they want that—a world with no consequences—but it cuts both ways. Without consequences, none of our actions have any effect, good or bad. In a world with no consequences, we have no connection to anything and nothing matters." Jackson cleared his throat as he bordered uncomfortably close to philosophic.

"Consequences suck," Chandi declared petulantly.

"You ain't wrong, kid."

*****

After Jackson heard the news from another sentry, he allowed himself a measure of cautious relief and headed to bed. Tomorrow night was the Longest Night, and there would be little hope for sleep then. He found his door unexpectedly unlocked and a dim light spilling out from under the door. He put his hand on his dagger before pushing it open, but lowered his guard as he spied Cassie asleep in his bed. His work was pushed to one side of his table, making way for a covered plate, an empty pair of glasses, and a bottle of champagne on his table.

The sorcerer took off his gear as quietly as he could, but fatigue made his fingers clumsy. He cursed as he dropped a sachet of ball bearings and Cassie stirred. "Don't you have your own room to sleep in?" Jackson teased as she yawned and rubbed the sleep from her eyes.

"I came here to see you and thought I would just wait, but I must have fallen asleep." Cassie stretched her arms out and caught a first look at Jackson. His shoulders were slumped, dark circles hung under his eyes, and deep lines of worry still furrowed his face. "You look world weary. And old."

He took a seat by the table. "Had to give a kid a pep talk."

Cassie shook her head—two things he wasn't great with: kids and inspirational speeches. "You need a drink," she declared.

"Save the bubbly. I've got something better suited to the job." He grabbed a bottle of whiskey from a shelf and poured two. "What brings you to Unseen Waters in the middle of a barbarian invasion?" he affected polite levity with just the right dose of sarcasm.

Cassie typically played her cards close to her chest, but there was something tired and sincere in his voice. "I wanted to go home for Longest Night, get away from politics for a few days. Only problem is that I didn't have anywhere to go. I figured Khiri's here, Ry's here, you're here—this is as close to home as I'm going to get." Jackson held his tongue and nodded out of respect for her candor.

She quickly changed the subject. "As soon as I heard about the wastelanders, I wanted to check up on you, make sure you were okay," she alluded to—without directly citing—his massacred family.

Jackson didn't move or change his gaze. "I've been living with those ghosts for a long time, Cassie."

"I know, but Ry happened to mention that you weren't

sleeping and were pulling extra shifts—"

"Ry has a habit of exaggerating," Jackson replied. *And a real problem keeping his mouth shut*, he finished the sentence in his head as he finished his drink.

"I brought some food, in case you had skipped dinner," Cassie offered without pressure or suggestion. Jackson's stomach growled as he pulled off the cloth. His mouth watered as he bit into the sandwich, and he couldn't stop himself from taking another bite. She snooped around this room in plain sight; it felt less silly than watching him eat.

"Word just came in—the king's combined forces defeated the wastelanders, and most of our troops should be back in a few days," he relayed the news after he polished off his plate.

"That's great news. Why do you sound suspicious?"

"I don't like anything I can't confirm. Trust but verify," Jackson quoted the ancients. Cassie smiled, *I taught him that one*.

"I guess I'd better get to my own room." Cassie sighed and rose from his bed. "Jackson, try to get some sleep tonight, okay?" She was about to close the door when she heard him call her name. Cassie paused and stepped back in.

"Thanks," was all he said.

She gave him a nod. "May you find the stillness in the night," she bid softly before closing the door behind her.

*****

The trek southwest was cold and hungry as most of their supplies had been destroyed in the ambush. The only uninjured were those in the very back of the line who'd escaped Dexter's trap. Left only with what they were carrying on them during the march to Gouvernear, the tattered remains of the Laughter at the End of Time trudged closer to the ruins, where they could lick their wounds and carve out a place to survive. Under Terem's leadership, they avoided detection that would bring down Dexter's wrath upon them. As they moved deeper into Watertown, they found their feet and their flagging spirits rose. They felt at home among the skeletal husks of the ancients.

In this renewed spirit, some wanted to waylay the lone rider, speeding through the ruins at night. Maybe he would have some food to tide them over until they could hunt and trap? But it was Terem's hand that stayed them. "How much food could one sentient carry?" he reasoned. "Let's see where he is heading."

Chapter Seventeen

The Monastery of Unseen Waters buzzed with activity as the morning of Longest Night dawned. As word spread about the defeated muties, the adults' moods lightened considerably and the students caught wind of the lurking danger that could have been. The daily routines were observed, but the underlining anticipation for the holiday colored every aspect of the day and seemed infectious. Cook put a little extra sweetener and spices in the morning porridge, Dendra threw down fewer nettles in her station, and Tenets of Faith became story time about the historical roots of Longest Night and the different ways the ancients would celebrate and co-op the winter solstice to suit their cultural or religious needs.

It was a countdown to dinner, when the celebration unofficially started with a feast in the dining hall—the only communal area Lucy was allowed to decorate since it wasn't explicitly a religious space like the main hall. Church observation began later that evening, when the abbess led an evening meditation and lit the fire that was to burn until morning. The entire monastery kept vigil, feeding the flames through the night. Brothers and sisters of the stride would drift in and out throughout the night, some slipping away for amusement, others for a few hours of shuteye, but most took the opportunity for fellowship: to stay up late, play games, make music, dance, stoke the fire, drink too much cider, and eat too many sweets. At sunrise, the faithful ushered in the new year with morning devotion.

The entire monastery was given New Year's Day for private reflection, which essentially meant a day off work—no training, no chores, no teaching, no paperwork—truly an auspicious way to start the new year. Even the kitchen staff were given the day off, which led to extreme food preparation in the days leading up to Longest Night. Small pies and bites with plenty of rolls were the food of choice for New Year's Day, as they could be assembled en masse beforehand and left out for people to eat at their leisure without leaving a mountain of dishes to be washed the next day. There were no idle hands in the kitchen, and the oven wouldn't grow cold until the Longest Night came and went.

The soft light in the dining hall twinkled off the glitz and glitter of the dangling ornaments staggered above everyone's heads. Garlands draped the walls from wreath to wreath. The tantalizing smells from the kitchen wetted everyone's appetite as the first cask of cider was opened. The residents and guests of Unseen Waters developed a rosy glow from the warmth of the hearth, the convivial company, and the feast laid out before them: roasted nuts, candied fruit, slices of roasted meats, pastry-wrapped cheese, and loaves of bread with an array of spreads. The Order of the Guard joined the monastery for dinner, taking shifts in their own vigil on the walls.

As the night deepened, the brothers and sisters of the stride convened in the main hall. The dim light from the braziers caught the fragrant smoke from the burning incense that filled the faithful's nostrils as the prayer wheel was spun. The mother of the stride, bedecked in her ceremonial robes, stepped upon the dais and addressed them. It had been a trying year, and it seemed disingenuous not to acknowledge it in her remarks, but it was hardly the focus of her sermon. She spoke of the importance of seeking the true path, even if it is beset with challenges. She called upon the bonds that held them together in stillness. She advised them to leave the obstacles of this year before crossing into the next. She beseeched them to be the beacon of still light under the shattered moon, pure and unyielding in its brilliance. She ended the sermon as every Church of Parkour did on this night, "Light shines brightest in the darkness of night."

The prayer wheel was spun again as she guided them through the litany of stillness: stillness of the body, stillness of the eyes, stillness of breath, and stillness of the mind. A quiet energy permeated the room as each phase was marked with a high-pitched chime. In the stillness, a spark ignited a fire bundle that the mother of the stride carried outside, shielding it from the wind. Her brothers and sisters of the stride followed to the stack of dry wood built in the courtyard earlier that day to receive the holy flame. As Khiri brought the bundle to the kindling, the dried leaves and crumpled paper hungrily took the flame. Smoke curled into the sky as the dancing fingers of white, yellow, orange, red, and blue flames consumed the parched logs.

Cinnamon and clove filled the air from the mulled cider simmering in a large caldron, ready to warm those determined to stay outside. The crackle of the fire was soon joined by the pulsing tempo as sentients cobbled together a percussion band in the glow of the blaze. Finn pulled out his harmonica and another girl a wooden flute, and soon a melody wound its way into song. Some had already taken to dancing, but Chandi needed more cider before that was going to happen. As she waited in line, she caught Mika wailing away on a handheld drum, whipping the double-sided mallet in his right hand.

The music came to a lull and the players changed when she nudged him with mug. "I didn't know you played the drums."

"I'm more than a pretty face and a good runner," he teased as his eyes mischievously hinted that more could be said but wasn't. As the music started, he grabbed her hand. "Come on, let's dance." She found herself swaying in his arms before she could answer and found she no longer wanted to object.

"Best part of year?" Mika asked over the music.

Chandi thought about it—it had been an eventful year. If she were being honest, it was running with the tracers in

Oswego, but that was hardly something she could tell Mika about. "Making pathfinder," she fibbed slightly, but her reason rang true, "I feel like I finally got to start doing what I was meant to do. What about you?"

Mika screwed his face. "Tough call. I'd have to say getting radiation poison."

She elbowed him. "It's not nice to kid."

"Who's joking?" Chandi blushed and tried to look away, but stopped when she felt his fingertips on her face. As she looked up, he softly kissed her lips. "Happy Longest Night." Before Chandi could reply, an alarm sounded from the sentry on the wall.

*****

It was all so clear to Terem—the Church of Parkour weren't fighters. They always ran away from conflict in Ottawa, protected by their mercenaries and President de Frontenac's troops. All they had to do was take out the soldiers and all the winter stores behind the walls were theirs. His plan was simple—attack the barracks at night when the bulk would be sleeping. Without their soldiers, taking the monastery would only be a matter of time.

Terem marshaled the mere hundred that remained out of the thousand that marched out of Ottawa. They had survived raids and ambushes, frozen river crossings, the weather, and the vagaries of fate. They were the strongest by all measures—they were still standing. He stood before them, before battle, and gave a speech loquacious by mutie standards. "We are the Laughter at the End of Time. Starvation, deprivation, and defeat is not how we live nor how we will die. Rise up with me! If they do not let us in, we will knock the door down!" He waved his bazooka in the air.

They descended on the barracks, expecting to cut down unconscious sentients in their beds. Terem could not have known that more than half the bunks would be empty and that the soldiers within would be partially armored and armed due to the skeleton crew conditions. The numbers were still on their side, but the contest was more than they'd bargained for. When the fighting spilled outside, the bullets from the guards on the wall were to be expected, but he could not have foreseen that the monastery was no ordinary church installation, as the panel moved and the plasma gun in the wall started firing searing red bolts.

The wild-eyed man they had picked up outside of Ottawa began to chant in an incomprehensible tongue. He was not one of them, but he followed in their wake of destruction. None dared to kill him as he spoke to the dead, and no one risked the wrath of the otherworld. Terem was pretty sure he was crazy—it was something in his eyes, and it wasn't the fact that one was blue and one was brown. The wind picked up as his voice swelled, tearing a rift in the veil marked by an electrical storm that charged the air itself. A black figure emerged from an arc of lightning; the man cackled in glee at the spirit made flesh.

*****

The courtyard stirred with movement after the alarm sounded: the monastery was under attack. They gathered in the main hall within the sigil pillars where the abbess handed out orders. Pathfinders-in-training were to corral the tenderfoots and novices in the main hall and lead the ritual of bounds. Everyone else was to prepare for battle until further notice. The abbess moved to gather more information on what was happening outside the walls while Ariadne joined the effort to get the students to safety.

The front gates were already closed and reinforced, and the sentries took aim at the enemy from the wall. Ryland grabbed his rifle and ammo to pick off as many as he could, and his trusty pistol was tucked into a shoulder holster. Jackson joined him, fully kitted out and ready to fight. His crossbow may been low tech, but its bolts could still be deadly. The muttering from the otherworld accelerated and crescendoed in Jackson's ears until he felt a rip in the veil. The bolts of lightning that filled the sky were not natural, and he quickly consulted the spirits on what was coming through. They clamored to speak to him, offering their knowledge and spells for a small piece of him. He struck his bargain for a name—the eternal, spirit of destruction.

The gauzy black figure that emerged from a streak of lightning chilled everyone's heart, regardless of their affiliation. Its inky form seemed unending as it dove in and out of battle, rending bodies and absorbing the screams of the dying with each pass. Ryland emptied his magazine into the wretched creature, yelling at Jackson, "Got any ideas?"

Jackson grabbed the carved horn from his belt and gathered the quiet stillness in his mind amidst the chaos of battle. He started his incantation, calling upon the spirits of light and life, of battle and valor. He brought the horn to his lips and blew forcefully. A sonic wave rolled out, knocking the sentients below to the ground. A ball of light fell from the sky and many still argue about what they saw that night. Some say a winged angelic figure struck down the boundless ebony form with a giant sword. Others saw a warrior maiden pierce the creature's heart with her spear. Then there were those that saw a golden chariot's rider lasso the perpetual darkness and drag it into the ground. Their hearts lightened with the absence of the unfathomable blackness and Ryland was about to crack a joke when another streak of light sailed into the air, this time from the ground.

Chapter Eighteen

The eight pathfinders-in-training stood dumbstruck. One minute, they were dancing and drinking by the bonfire, the next they were under attack. As the gravity of the situation sunk in, Yan was the first to speak. "We need to make sure everyone is here. The novices should be able to take attendance of their pods, and the oldest of the tenderfoots should know the count of their numbers."

Willem and Joshi kept everyone within the pillars while Chandi looked for Sura; while she was no longer a tenderfoot, she was the oldest and most likely to notice if anyone was missing. Natalie and Mira spread the word among the novices—let us know if someone is unaccounted for, and we will find them. Willem wanted to close the doors immediately, but Finn pointed out that others who were not at the bonfire might still be coming. Even as he spoke, a trickle of scholars entered and help calm the younger students. Chandi breathed a sigh of relief when she spotted Bartholomew among the crowd.

Once they verified that all the tenderfoots and novices were present, Finn and Jukka shut the doors of the main hall, dulling the sounds of combat that leaked through. The pillars would protect them from otherworldly attacks, but it would do little against wastelanders. The eight of them positioned themselves around the main hall: one at each pillar and at the midpoint between pillars. Even though it had been years since their running days, the present scholars fortified their ranks; the ritual of bounds was an old practice. Yan spun the prayer wheel to focus their flitting minds. Chandi closed her eyes and found her center, expanding the tranquil quiet as she repeated the mantra in her mind. *This is the wall of our stillness. None but friend shall pass.*

*****

The eternal was terrifyingly majestic and the Laughter at the End of Time cheered at its arrival, feeling akin to the darkness. With each graceful swoop, it devoured all the life it could grasp in its spectral tendrils, and the man with different-colored eyes reveled in the destruction until he was run through with a sword. The madman laughed as the black specter came and devoured its fading liberator.

Terem hacked and hewed his way through the Order of the Guard, taking note of how many of his comrades fell from the plasma gun. Its lethal bolts were cutting them down with precision. The blare of a horn sounded over the din, knocking Terem off his feet. The descending flash blinded him momentarily, and when his vision returned, the eternal was gone. Heartened by this turn, the Order of the Guard on the ground rallied.

Terem took a knee, loaded his weapon, hoisted it upon his shoulder, and aimed for the section of wall under the plasma gun. He had hoped to save the bazooka for the front gates in case there was resistance, but if he didn't take out that gun, it would be a moot point. With an explosive whoosh, the missile flew into the air. His ears were still ringing as he dropped the launcher and grabbed the nearest melee weapon.

*****

The stone crumbled from under Jackson's feet as the wall shuddered upon impact. Ryland screamed out as he saw his friend and another sentry fall in the rockslide. The light from the bonfire cut through the billow of dust as the tinker-runner bound down; the pile would have been precarious to most, but was of little consequence to a tracer of the true path. Ryland checked the wounded for signs of life. Both were free of the debris and still breathing, but unconscious.

"Jackson!" Cassie yelled across the courtyard. "Ry, is he alive?"

"Still breathing, but knocked out," he tersely answered, unburying what was left of the plasma gun.

She brushed the blood and dirt from Jackson's face. "Should we move him?"

Ryland found his quarry. "We should kill whatever comes through that gap." Tools manifested in his hands as he unscrewed the casing and starting working on the damaged sections. He was spitting out parts so fast, Cassie could see the tiny black mites form tech before moving to the next one. They made her teeth itch.

Cassie stiffened her resolve. "You fix that, I'll buy you some time."

"Much appreciated," he answered as his nanites melded a lighter into the panel.

Cassie was no tracer of the true path, but she had learned a thing or two in her time at Unseen Waters. She scaled the pile, ten feet tall at its peak. Her voice bellowed into the night as she broke off a length of silk thread from a spool and held it taut between her fingers. Her spell whipped the sky into a frenzy as she chanted in the language of the otherworld. The thread ignited; her offer had been accepted. A band of skeletal warriors rose from the ground and bowed to their mistress. She commanded them to attack all who did not bear the sign of the Church of Parkour and they rushed to obey.

Khiri regarded her sisters and brother of the stride by the flames: her faithful prioress, her four instructors, three visiting tracers, and four tracers-in-training. "We have a breech in the wall, and we must act if we want Unseen Waters to see the morning. The Order of the Guard is outnumbered but still fighting. We will assist as we can and move as one in stillness.

Not one mutie will enter our walls. Let us flow like water over the land and wash the filth that has blown on our doorstep."

The sept of thirteen glided up and over the rocks and onto the battlefield, shadows bouncing from point to point. Khiri led with Ariadne, the tracers and three instructors guarding the flank. In the rear, Netu released Umbra from his flesh and the giant spider skittered beside him. Nestled in the center were the tracers-in-training, the least developed in their skill but capable in their own right. They vaulted, climbed, jumped, and tumbled through the ruins until they were in the thick of battle. They intercepted attacks, and when the muties struck, the faithful turned their aggression back on them. *As it is written, so it is run.*

Ariadne spun and threw out a web, entangling the axe-wielding barbarian aiming for the abbess. Zera drew a spark from within and lit it on fire. The immolating warrior drew attention to their sept. Dendra threw out a barbed lash, pulling the charging spearman down to the rubble while a tracer pinned him to the ground with his own weapon. Bibi dropkicked a marksman in the back taking aim at Aren, while Aka's large fist punched the gunman into unconsciousness. The sound of gunfire rang out from all sides and Sabine flattened his quills and shielded himself from projectiles while he extended his claws. Lars was startled when a skeletal warrior deflected a blow in his favor, but as it wasn't attacking the Order of the Guard or his brothers and sisters of the stride, he left well enough alone.

There were enough enemies without creating more.

*****

Terem fumed as his plan disintegrated before him. He disengaged from combat and maneuvered behind the field of combat, making a beeline for the hole he had created in the wall. The Church of Parkour had taken Ottawa from him; he would destroy Watertown for them! He took a hit on his shoulder from a sentry's longarm, but he persisted. He was no longer concerned with his survival, only vengeance.

He reached the breech in the wall and climbed, stumbling on the sliding rocks. His right hand became slick with his own blood, but his fury pushed him on. Terem was almost at the top when a lone figure greeted him, wielding a strange-looking weapon. The pulse of plasma burned through him and he dropped to his knees before face-planting dead into the debris.

"Cutting it a bit close, weren't you?" Cassie commented from the side.

"He didn't make it in, did he?" Ryland shot back. "It's not like this thing was designed to be fired like this."

"Yeah, I'm not sure how you used a yo-yo to fix it."

"I didn't ask when you raised a skeleton army," he pointed out.

"I guess some mysteries are better left unsolved," Cassie concluded.

*****

This is the wall of our stillness. None but friend shall pass. This is the wall of our stillness. None but friend shall pass, Chandi repeated over and over again. She had lost track of time when she felt a hand on her shoulder. *No one should be able to break through, unless…* Chandi opened her eyes and saw Ryland, covered in dirt but in one piece. She impulsively hugged him and held on for dear life. "Is it over?"

Ryland leaned in and patted her back. "The worst of it is, but there are a lot of wounded. They are going to need you in the infirmary, and a lot of fresh water as they start bringing everyone in. I need you to fetch both your pearls so they can start boiling water."

Chandi shook her head and left the great hall. It was dark and the bonfire was still burning but dwindling down. She got both her freshwater pearl and her pearl of making and made a stop in the kitchen for the largest container with a lid she could find. The staff was already stoking the fires to boil the water. Chandi dropped her freshwater pearl in and tightly closed the cap, explaining that it had to be done each time water was poured out, or it would flood.

The first of the injured were already in the infirmary when she entered. She washed her hands, put on a clean apron, and went to work. The bodies spilled into the hallway until other rooms could be repurposed. Chandi went from room to room, washing wounds, quenching parched throats, and replenishing the fresh water supply at each station. Each time she passed the bank of windows, the bonfire had gotten a little smaller, and the night a little less dark.

Chapter Nineteen

The ground between the monastery and the barracks was littered with bodies. Aren's soldiers conducted the mercy killings and flagged down assistance from Khiri's sept to get those not mortally wounded to the infirmary in the monastery. All total, twenty-two members of the Order of the Guard surrendered their tabards that night, with another thirty-three wounded. The mother of the stride gave a benediction to those who'd sacrificed their lives in service to the church, bidding them reincarnation to a higher form befitting their valor.

The seven pathfinders-in-training were called to help move the dead and scavenge the battlefield, with so many fallen to consider—nearly a hundred wastelanders by estimation. The scene seemed unreal as they crested the rock pile, like it was a painting instead of real life. Three of them vomited as soon as they waded into the carnage. Mira, who was raised in a family of butchers and was no stranger to handling freshly killed flesh, was just glad the cold mitigated the smell.

The Order of the Guard opted to handle their dead in their way, leaving them in cold conditions until the returning squads arrived to help bury them. There was discussion on what to do with the wastelanders' bodies. While there was a giant bonfire in the courtyard, no one suggested burning them there—that was a sacred fire that none would defile with the dead. Although the ground wasn't frozen yet, digging a mass grave would take days with current resources. Ultimately, it was decided that their corpses would be searched and hauled away from the monastery, to decompose the natural way and feed the scavengers of the ruins.

Willem discovered his knack for finding treasures was not limited to the ruins. He seemed to intuit every hidden pouch, inner pocket, or false shoe bottom. Sometimes the items clearly had monetary worth, while other things were useful. Then there were pieces that must be of sentimental value, as Willem couldn't see any inherent value or utility. Still, he collected them and added them to the processing bag.

This gruesome work had, to a certain degree, inured Willem to the death around him, but the next corpse gave him pause. The gaping hole in his chest was par for the course, but the wastelander's face horrified the pathfinder. His tongue lolled out and his eyes were open, bulging from their sockets. His right eye was blue and his left was brown, but that is not why Willem found him so grotesque. Throughout the course of the night, Willem had seen many faces of the dying, with expressions of agony, surprise, pleading, and surrender. This face was grinning from ear to ear, a countenance joyously embracing the otherworld, almost in mockery of life itself.

Willem shuttered and got to work. He patted down the robes and found the usual supplies, but stopped to investigate when he felt something square and hard sewn into the lining. Willem pulled out a knife and ripped the fabric. The small metallic cube felt light in his hands and reflected the bright moonlight at various angles. Each facet was intricately etched. Willem shook it gently and heard something rattle inside. He twisted, pried, and levered each side to no avail—the cube remained shut. The familiar rhythmic thump of the handcart cut his investigation short, but not his curiosity. Willem quickly stuffed the cube in his pocket as Finn and Joshi hoisted the next load of corpses.

*****

Sunrise wasn't far away by the time Chandi took a seat in the courtyard. The dead had been accounted for, the wounded brought in, and the Monastery of Unseen Waters still stood despite the hole in her side. She was so tired that it hadn't dawned on her that she still had the pearl of making clutched in her hand. *You really came in handy today*, she thought as she rolled it in her palm. The last of the moonlight fell upon it while the bonfire cast shadows of her fingers across the pearl. Suddenly, the gray pearl gleamed with a soft diffuse light from within. Chandi was so awestruck that she didn't hear the footsteps behind her.

"I think tonight lived up to its name," Lucy spoke and handed Chandi a mug of something warm and cheerful. Chandi reflexively closed her hand. Lucy saw the astonished look on her face. "Are you okay, Chandi?"

Chandi's surprised mind raced. "Lucy, I need you to tell me what you see in my hand and promise that you won't freak out." Lucy nodded. "And promise that you won't tell anybody, like *really* promise."

"Chandi, you're starting to scare me, and we just survived a mutie invasion."

"I'm serious, Lucy. Promise?"

Lucy straightened up and put on her serious face. "I promise." Chandi closed her eyes and slowly opened up her hand. Lucy gasped. "Is that the pearl the octopus guy gave you? It's gorgeous. And huge!" Chandi opened her eyes and saw the pearl of making, sans glow. "Mind if I hold it?"

"Sure," Chandi replied, confused. She watched Lucy turn it in the light before handing it back. Still nothing. Chandi stuffed it into her pocket. *You aren't going insane. It was totally glowing*, she emphatically told herself.

"Oh, look what Willem gave me!" Lucy squealed as she dug under her shirt, producing the cameo. Chandi spent an appropriate amount of time admiring it. "I think I'm his girlfriend now."

"You aren't sure?"

"Well, he was in the middle of asking me when the alarm

rang, and he's been out scavenging the battlefield with the other pathfinders and tracers."

"So what will you tell him when he gets back?" Chandi let her curiosity supersede her tact.

Lucy shrugged. "Does it really matter what we call it? It is what it is…I'm crazy about him and he's crazy about me. Right now, we have each other. That's about as good as it gets." Lucy stoked the fire with a stick and another piece of charred wood fell and broke into ash. "But if it would make him feel better, then sure, I'll let him be my boyfriend."

Chandi laughed. "You are wiser than your years."

"So I've been told," she snidely remarked. "I'm going in to get some food before morning devotion. You coming?"

"In a little bit. Just want a little more time by the fire." Lucy's soft steps receded as Chandi stared at the dying fire, the fervent red glow of the embers. The sky was lightening in predawn, but the shattered moon was still visible. Chandi took the pearl of making out of her pocket and exhaled heavily as it dimly glowed in her hand. *It doesn't matter what you call it. It is what it is.*

*****

"Good morning, sunshine!" Ryland hailed as Jackson's eyes fluttered. "Well, technically it's still night, but it's still good to see you awake. You've been out for a couple of hours."

"What happened?" Jackson muttered and let out a yelp when he tried to sit up. "And why does everything hurt?"

"You took a pretty nasty bump on your head, so I'll give you the high points. The wastelanders came, they knocked a hole in the wall, and unfortunately you were standing right on top of it. But you pulled a badass spirit from your horn before the wall took you out and eventually we won. You're bruised and battered but nothing is broken, so as long as your concussion isn't more serious, you'll live."

"How do you know nothing's broken?"

"Because I x-rayed you," Ryland proclaimed proudly.

"You what?! Ry, what have I told you me and tech!"

"Relax, you touched no tech and no nanites crawled over you in the process. Just a little radiation passed through you, and not enough to give you cool powers," Ryland reassured him as he stood up. His ragged face belied his cheerful tone. "I have to take care of some things before morning devotion, but I leave you in capable hands."

Before Jackson could ask, Cassie came into the room with a tray of food and a pitcher of water. "How are you feeling?"

"Like the can in a long game of kick the can."

Cassie smiled. "Your head injury can't be too bad if you can make jokes."

"You know what would really help? A glass of whiskey."

"Absolutely not," she said firmly, pouring him a glass of water. "You're under observation for the next day or two to make sure there isn't more injury to the brain, which means no alcohol until you're in the clear."

Jackson groaned. "And what am I supposed to do about the pain?"

"Just be glad you are human and the ancients' pain medication still works on you." She put two white circular tablets in his hand with a glass of water. "It won't take it away, but it should help."

Jackson choked down the pills. Chalky, yet…nope, just chalky.

"You have to tell me if you feel"—she pulled out her notebook—"nauseated, confused, experience changes in vision, or have a really bad headache."

Amused, Jackson inquired wryly, "And what are you supposed to do?" He hadn't seen this side of Cassie before—stern caretaker.

"I'm supposed to make sure you don't lose consciousness again for long periods of time now that you are awake, and watch for signs that you aren't thinking straight or being yourself." She closed her notebook. "And, you know, help you do stuff?" she added uncertainly.

"Doesn't sound like a very fun vacation for you." Jackson picked up a pie from the plate.

Cassie shrugged as she fluffed his pillows and helped him sit up. "Still better than babysitting the elder council." She sat next to him and produced a deck of cards. "Now, get ready for an epic game of cards and if you prove to be mentally undamaged, we can make this interesting," she said, pulling out and shaking a pouch of coins.

*****

Khiri stayed out as long as she could to oversee her brothers and sisters of the stride search through the vestiges of violence. She would have liked to have spared them, but the world under the shattered moon does not always allow such indulgences. As the wounded were brought in and the dead taken deeper into the ruins, the only signs of what transpired were the breeched wall and the freezing viscera and blood that seeped into the ground. To his credit, Aren stayed close by, making sure all his soldiers were accounted for before going inside to have his wounds assessed.

But sunrise would come soon enough, and she needed to ready herself for morning devotion, which waited for no one. Khiri changed out of her blood-spattered robes and washed herself with clean water; it finally ran clear after the third basin. She repeated the mantra of forgiveness in her mind until her heart was rid of anger, hatred, and vengeance. *They did what they do, just like I do what I must.*

The tigress was straightening her vestments when she heard a knock on her door. On any other day, such an early visitor would have been remarkable, but she was still genuinely surprised when she opened the door. "Chandi, what are you doing here? It's almost time for morning devotion."

The pathfinder bowed before answering, "It won't take long, but I wanted to talk to you before things got busy with the cleanup and repairs."

"Certainly. Come in, sister of the stride." Khiri stepped aside, granting Chandi entrance before shutting the door. "What's on your mind?"

Chandi took a deep breath and began, "I want to stay at Unseen Waters and continue training. I was born to run. I also want to use my gifts to heal sentients, and I don't mind doing that on behalf of the church in exchange for the continuation of benefits for my family and village, but I have conditions." Chandi looked to the abbess to see if she had any comment, but Khiri merely nodded. "I don't want to be called away so often or so far that it interrupts my training. Once I'm a tracer, any trips I make on behalf of the church count toward my travel quota. Lastly, I want a visitation allowance to see my family. Now that I am no longer a child, there isn't a reason for the church to prohibit contact."

Khiri regarded her once ward; there was a steeliness in her green eyes, hard like emeralds. "I'm glad to hear that you would like to stay," she started. "However, in a negotiation, I must represent the church's interest. Brother Bartholomew was quite the advocate before he turned his focus on scholarship; perhaps he would be willing to help you draft a document of your requests for consideration." Chandi bowed again and made for the door before her bluster left her. "Chandi, out of curiosity, how did you come to this decision?"

Normally, Chandi would have clammed up, but somewhere between her exhaustion and exhilaration, she found she didn't care what the abbess thought about her reasons. She had clarity about what she wanted, and it felt amazing. "I am who I am. I don't have to choose which parts of me to alter or ignore to suit the church's labels. If Ryland can run and tinker, if Cassandra can see the bias and still advise the elder council, if Jackson can do whatever he does without getting in trouble for it, then I can just be me and that's enough."

"I see. Thank you for your candor. You'd better get moving, the morning is fast approaching." As the door closed behind Chandi, Khiri's stoic mien broke into a smile.

Chandi breathed a sigh of relief from the other side of the door. As the adrenaline wore off, she replayed the scene in her head. Had she really just told the Church of Parkour to take it or leave it? No. She told them "this is who I am and you would be a fool to stop it," because she was willing to stay as long as it worked for her, too. She fought the urge to skip her way down the hall, but there was a swagger in her gait. As she walked through the courtyard, she caught the fading image of the shattered moon and felt a pang of pity. *Moonstone, what have they done to you?*

*****

The mother of the stride left her office and entered the courtyard. The horizon gleamed, heralding the incipient sunrise. She drew the fire starters from her sleeve and buried the tips into the cinders of the bonfire. The new year would rise from the ashes of the last, like a soaring phoenix.

She entered the main hall, whose doors were cast open, inviting all the brothers and sisters of the stride to congregate. Some still bore the traces of last night, but all that were able were present for morning devotion. It waited for no one.

The abbess lit the incense and blew out the flame; its fragrant smoke unfurled. As the tigress sat upon the dais, a hush fell over the faithful. The peel of the gong echoed throughout the room, followed by the rattle of the prayer wheel.

"Stillness of the body," Khiri spoke. They assumed the posture of meditation while the chime rang.

"Stillness of the eyes," she instructed as she softened her gaze; gone were the piercing pupils of the night before. She closed her eyes as the second ping passed.

"Stillness of breath." The room collectively breathed in and out, exhaling through the third ring.

"Stillness of the mind." The abbess ushered the Monastery of Unseen Waters into stillness once more as they meditated together until the prayer wheel ceased to drone.

THE END

Chandi will next appear in *Chandi and the Black Diamond*

www.ingramcontent.com/pod-product-compliance
Lightning Source LLC
Chambersburg PA
CBHW030225180626
46810CB00008B/2978